2

4

SHELTER FROM THE STORM

Also by Tony Dunbar

DELTA TIME
AGAINST THE GRAIN
HARD TRAVELING (WITH LINDA KRAVITZ)
OUR LAND TOO

• • •

THE TUBBY DUBONNET MYSTERIES

TRICK QUESTION
CITY OF BEADS
CROOKED MAN

TONY DUNBAR

SHELTER
FROM THE
STORM

G. P. PUTNAM'S SONS
New York

This book is fiction. All of the characters and settings are
purely imaginary. There is no Tubby Dubonnet and the real
New Orleans is different from his make-believe city.

G. P. Putnam's Sons
Publishers Since 1838
a member of Penguin Putnam Inc.
200 Madison Avenue
New York, NY 10016

Library of Congress Cataloging-in-Publication Data

Dunbar, Anthony P.
Shelter from the storm / Tony Dunbar.
p.   cm.
ISBN 0-399-14301-7
I. Title.
PS3554.U46336S48   1997   97-10844   CIP
813'.54—dc21

Printed in the United States of America
1   3   5   7   9   10   8   6   4   2

This book is printed on acid-free paper. ∞

Book design by Jennifer Ann Daddio

ACKNOWLEDGMENTS

I gratefully acknowledge the professional advice of two men of the sea, Amby Daigre and Sam Abelar; the musical knowledge of Doug "A" Jackson, Michael Blackmon, and Mischa Philippoff; the Mardi Gras smarts of Janie Baum and Stephen Nicaud; the defense of Chicago cooking by Lauri Lentz; and the helpful comments of a faithful and critical reader, Linda Kravitz.

TO MY SISTER, LINDA LEE

SHELTER FROM THE STORM

1

"They had this place tore up the last time I was here," Monk griped to Big Top as he drove under the rectangular green sign that said New Orleans International Airport. "And they still got it tore up. No telling which way we're supposed to go." A cement truck rumbled past them on the right, raining gravel on the windshield of their Chevy Astro minivan.

Big Top jerked his freckled elbow inside for protection, concerned about the cars madly crisscrossing lanes around them. Riding in the high-up front seat made all the other cars look much closer.

He saw some instructions ahead.

"Arriving Flights," Big Top said helpfully, pointing. An old Chrysler with dented tail fins narrowly missed the front bumper and swerved into the next lane.

"Jesus of Nazareth!" Monk hollered, and banged his fist on the horn.

The Chrysler careened off into Short-Term Parking. A skinny white arm came over the roof and shot them the bird.

Monk gunned the van's engine malevolently and rolled

down into the dark bowels of the lower-level baggage claim area.

A big cop in a rumpled blue uniform screamed, "SLOW IT DOWN!" in Monk's face, and he obediently hit the brakes. Big Top had to grab the dashboard to keep from going through the glass. He and Monk exhaled in unison as the van crawled through the snarl of cabs, limousines, and cars meeting passengers.

"See him?" Big Top asked. "I ain't never met Rue."

"No, I don't," Monk said, fighting for a spot at the curb. He had met Rue and was afraid of him. "He's a little guy though," Monk said, "and mean as a snake," as if you could spot the meanness in somebody.

Willie LaRue, or "Rue," as he liked to be called, walked a straight path from Delta's Gate 31 on Concourse A all the way through the maelstrom of congested humanity to the main terminal. Though his eyes darted constantly from side to side, his head barely seemed to move, and he avoided collisions with the people hurrying toward the rest rooms and parents herding children mainly by suddenly slowing down or speeding up his pace. He wore a brown straw cowboy hat, brim turned down, with a green headband, and he had pink ears that stuck straight out like wings on a dead chicken. He had on a tan leisure suit, with dark brown trim, and looked like lots of other Texas tourists getting off the Southwest Airlines flight.

LaRue carried a dull burgundy overnight bag in his left hand. That was all the luggage he needed. Everything else was supposed to be in the van, unless Monk or his hillbilly partner from Mississippi had forgotten to bring it.

New Orleans music seeped out of the intercom. At the moment, it was Fats Domino singing, "I am the sheik of Araby. Your love belongs to me." The chipper melody did not add any bounce to Rue's steps. His was a rigid composure that wouldn't crack. A kid on a leash dashed out in front of the thin man, lollipop embedded in wet purple lips. LaRue snarled and stepped over him.

His flight from Houston had been on time. He was right on schedule. Now, if the turnips from the boonies were where they were supposed to be, everything would be fine.

Marguerite Patino checked her straw-colored hair carefully in the noisy ladies' room on Concourse B. She finished by giving herself a big wink with her long black eyelashes and stepped briskly into the bright corridor swirling with people. Trailing a red plastic suitcase that rolled erratically on its tiny wheels, she promenaded toward the terminal, demurely deflecting the glances of all sorts of guys headed toward the planes.

She looked sharp. Her hair was permed into a reckless swirl of ringlets that Don, before he socked her for sixty dollars, had told her were just the thing for "down South." Her coral-pink suit came with the shortest skirt she owned and hung tightly on a body trimmed of most of its excess fat by three miserable weeks of fasting and aerobic agony. She was ready to get on with her first real vacation since a high-octane trip to Cancún two years ago with her ex-boyfriend Romney.

Her only regret was that her soul mate, Rondelle, was not along. Rondelle had come up with the idea of going to Mardi Gras in the first place. "Just the girls," she said, and she had even made the reservations. Then Rondelle had chickened out. They had had a big argument. Marguerite's lips turned down in a pout when she thought about it. Rondelle just could not seem to take the big leap. So she was stuck back in Chicago scraping ice off her Geo and Marguerite was here in New Orleans, ready to party down on Bourbon Street at the Mardi Gras. Only thing was, she had had to lie to her mother about traveling alone.

What's done is done. I'm thirty-one. Whoopee. She passed by the line of people trudging through the metal detector and entered the main terminal. Anticipating bacchanalia, she was immediately disappointed that it looked pretty much like a miniature version of the airport back home. The sight of something called an oyster bar and a tough-looking female concessionaire in fishnet stockings pushing a rolling wagon of whiskey bottles gave her some reassurance.

Past the baggage claim she stepped through the sliding glass doors into the Big Easy and immediately needed oxygen. Hot wet air wrapped around her like the steam of a sauna. Gasping, momentarily dizzy, she reached for a grimy concrete pillar for support.

"Taxi, ma'am? Right here." The short Lebanese had her elbow and was directing her, with charming courtesy, toward his vast cab labeled, in flowing gold script, the White Cloud. His purple shirt was half untucked from his tight black slacks, and his mustache was ragged. He looked very much like the cabbie who had dropped her off at O'Hare about three hours earlier.

Disoriented, Marguerite let herself be led away.

"That's our man." Monk pointed his chin at the tall figure with big ears emerging from the baggage area.

"Guess he knows us," Big Top mumbled as Willie LaRue, guided by some internal radar, stepped off the curb and pointed himself unerringly at the van.

"Skinny feller," Big Top said.

"He's a dangerous little prick. He's named for some damn cowboy, and he acts like it," Monk said, but he rolled down his window and called, "Hey, brother, join the party."

LaRue came alongside and lifted his sunglasses to examine the occupants of the van. His eyes were squinty and green and matched the band of his hat.

"You're Monk," he said by way of greeting.

"Right. We met before. This here is Big Top."

"Pleased to make your acquaintance," Big Top said.

LaRue made slits out of his eyes and nodded. Then he pulled the van's side door open loudly and vaulted himself into the back seat.

"Let's ride, boys," he said.

Monk pushed the buttons that rolled up the windows, and hit the air.

He steered around a party of locals carrying parkas and lugging their skis into the terminal, anxious to get out of town, and snaked through the traffic in the direction of daylight.

LaRue mopped his forehead with a handkerchief and turned around in his seat to inspect the van's cargo.

A brand-new turquoise five-horsepower Makita generator took up a lot of space in the rear and a handsome gray steel tool chest with enameled red drawers took up the rest.

"You got everything?" he asked doubtfully.

"The whole shopping list," Monk said, pointing the van toward the interstate. "You just gotta watch out the darkies don't steal everything out of it."

LaRue looked suspiciously at Monk, who was black as a buffalo horn, but he didn't say anything.

Big Top, who had a wave of unruly red hair over a face filled with freckles, giggled uncontrollably.

LaRue thought they were both idiots. He knew they lived in a house trailer way back in the pine trees somewhere in Mississippi, and he didn't care for that arrangement. Monk could pass for a college boy singing in a church choir, and he was said to be reliable, but his selection of Big Top, who resembled LaRue's own inbred cousins, was a major demerit.

"What you got for me?" he asked impatiently.

Big Top bent over to fish around under his seat and came up with a gun in a compact black nylon holster. He handed it butt-first over his shoulder to LaRue, who peeled back the Velcro strap and shook the weapon out for closer inspection.

"Forty-five caliber," Monk explained.

LaRue did not comment on the obvious but went to work figuring out how to fasten the holster to his belt.

"You don't worry someone will see that under your coat?" Big Top asked. "I keep mine in my boot."

"No," Rue replied. "I've been here before. Anyone sees a white man with a pistol on his belt in New Orleans, they figure him for a policeman."

Monk laughed. Big Top chewed gum.

At Metairie Road Monk flipped on the blinker and cruised off the exit ramp. He turned left into a cloud of black exhaust from a city bus.

"We'd better go by the back roads," he said as he set off on a roundabout route through potholed residential streets in the direction of Bayou St. John.

"You worried about a tail?" LaRue was tense.

"No, man," Monk said. "Damn parades are everywhere. They got 'em all over on Veterans this evening, and one of 'em goes down Canal Street this afternoon. Last week when I came down to look around I got stuck for an hour just trying to get across downtown. I could have locked up the van and parked in the middle of the street, but, you know, I didn't want to chance getting towed. So . . ." He swerved down a tree-lined street of two-story shotgun houses, white paint fading behind crooked iron fences. "We stick to the ol' hoods."

Some boys playing soccer with a beach ball jumped out of their path.

Abruptly, the narrow street joined a wide boulevard. They careened around a statue of Confederate General P.G.T. Beauregard, whose horse wore a bright bridle of plastic beads, and drove beside a wide, sluggish stream of water that had once provided passage to the tribes of Indians who traded with Frenchmen before being exterminated by them. A gentle grassy bank separated the roadway from the edge of the bayou. It being Sunday, solitary fishermen and urban picnickers claimed most of the shady spots along the shoreline. The setting was picturesque, and the people who lived in the expensive homes on the opposite bank had a relaxing view of tides rippling gently in and out, marred only by the occasional drunk or fleeing felon who missed a curve, went airborne, and ended up nose down in the ancient green muck.

"That's him," Monk said, pointing ahead to a smoky gray Pontiac parked beneath a spreading oak tree at water's edge. A tall and extremely thin dark-skinned man was leaning against the passenger door watching them approach. He fumbled around in the pocket of his khaki uniform shirt for a cigarette as the van crawled slowly past him on the jagged asphalt-and-clamshell shoulder and came to a halt in the grass.

Through the minivan's windows Willie LaRue studied the waiting man without saying anything.

The fellow finally got his cigarette lit, tossed a wooden match in the direction of the blue water, and slowly ambled in their direction. Monk stuck his head out the side window.

"Get in the back and let's talk," he directed.

The skinny man struggled with the sliding door, but he finally gave it a great pull with both hands and got it open.

"No smoking in here," LaRue ordered. He slid across the seat to make way for the newcomer.

The man was uncertain what to do with his cigarette. He took a big drag and laid his smoke carefully on the ground, where he hoped to retrieve it later. Crouching low, he poked the top half of his torso into the dark hold and pulled his legs in after him.

"Yo," he said to LaRue, who didn't reply. With a sigh, he strained to slam the door shut behind him and get his long legs properly arranged.

"This is James," Monk explained. "Security man at First Alluvial Bank. This is Big Top. This is Mr. Rue." He indicated with his index finger. All four men nodded. LaRue continued to adjust the pistol on his belt.

"Who's the other guy in your car?" Monk asked James, indicating the shadowy head in the Pontiac's passenger seat.

"That's Corelle," James said, shifting his weight to one side and grabbing his left calf with both hands to make himself secure.

"Why's he sitting out there instead of coming over to talk to us?"

"He wants me to do all the talking and work everything out," James said. "He's worried."

The afternoon glare coming through the windshield was bothering Monk, so he put on his sunglasses. He twisted around in his seat.

"What about?" Big Top asked anxiously.

"He thinks something may go wrong."

"Why don't we deal with Mr. Corelle's concerns later,"

Monk interrupted smoothly. "This man here is the boss," he said, indicating LaRue. "And he ain't got time for a lot of trash. Explain the plan to him."

"Sure. I work until two o'clock in the afternoon," James said. "Bank closes at noon 'cause it's the day before Mardi Gras. They'll be closed all day Tuesday for Mardi Gras and won't open until Wednesday morning."

"Right," Monk said. "And we're coming in with all our stuff at one o'clock tomorrow, right after lunchtime. Who's going to be there?"

"Nobody," James said with confidence. "All the secretaries and the bankers will be gone out of there before noon. Most of 'em don't even come in tomorrow, and them that do it's just to eat some King Cake and go home. It's a real slow day. They lock up the bank itself at twelve o'clock sharp. As soon as they clear all the customers out, the guard in the lobby gets to go home, too. Then I'll be all by myself."

"And you're going to get us into the vault?" Monk prompted.

"Not the vault, no, sir. Just the room with all the safe-deposit boxes."

"Well, that's what I meant." Monk looked at LaRue reassuringly. The boss flipped one of his earlobes back and forth with his fingertip and listened.

"Yes, sir," James continued. "That's my job. I sit in a little glass booth, see, right by where you go into the safe-deposit room. I can see the vault, but it's on a timer deal. I couldn't open it even if I knew the combination, and only Mr. Duplantier knows that. But with my monitors on I can see what's going on in the whole bank, upstairs, downstairs, and everywhere. I got keys to every door in the place. 'Cept the vault."

"We ain't interested in the vault," LaRue said. It was the first time he had spoken. "Just the safe-deposit boxes. And in not being disturbed."

"You ain't going to be disturbed while I'm there," James said, turning to face LaRue. He did not like the man's eyes and shifted his own to the straw hat. "Nobody's allowed to come down to the basement after the bank is closed. I've got it all locked off, and nobody is coming downstairs but you."

"We're using that generator behind you for the drills," Monk said. "It's mighty loud though. Is anybody going to hear it?"

"If they did, I don't believe anybody would care," James said. "I'm telling you, they're going home for Mardi Gras and they ain't stoppin' for nothin'."

LaRue held up his palm to stop Monk's interrogation. "You know the box number?" he asked James.

"Yes, sir." James's eyes were roaming all around the van, looking everywhere but at Rue, and he was sweating.

"Well, give it to me."

James handed Rue a crumpled-up piece of paper that he had hidden in the cuff of his trousers. LaRue took it and stuck it in his own pocket. "What happens when you go off shift in the afternoon?" he asked James.

The guard shuffled to reposition himself in the cramped back seat and grabbed his other leg.

"That's when Corelle comes on. He works from when I

get off until ten o'clock at night, and after he leaves, there won't be a soul around the place until Wednesday morning."

"The idea is," Monk explained, "we got all of tomorrow night and Tuesday to work. When we leave, we tie Corelle up to his chair and leave him there. His story will be that we broke in on him some way. If he gets fired, he is still sitting pretty because we can get him a new job with the city, plus he gets his fifty thousand."

"So why's he waiting out there in the car?" LaRue asked.

James rocked back and forth uneasily. Big Top, watching him, was getting dizzy.

"He says you guys are all getting away, and nobody knows I'm the one let you in, so I get away. He's the only one left behind for everybody to point at."

"His story," Monk said, "will be that he saw us beating on the bank's doors when he was making his rounds. He can make up any old thing. Like I was bleeding and begging him to help us. He can just say he opened the door a crack and we forced our way in."

"They'll fire him sure for that," James said.

Monk shrugged. "It's not much of a job, is it, James? What you get? Eight or nine dollars an hour? Twenty thousand a year? If the job was so great, you wouldn't be a part of this either."

"That's a fact," James agreed. "But I aim to keep the job anyway. Corelle is bound to lose his. I believe what's bothering him most, however, is he'll be tied up all Mardi Gras Day and he'll miss the parades and parties and whatnot." James laughed nervously, but nobody joined him.

LaRue looked sternly at Monk. "I thought all the details had already been worked out," he said quietly.

"Me too," Monk said. "It's too damn late for Corelle to be backing out," he told James.

Big Top reached around his seat and gave James's jumpy knee a squeeze. He popped his gum. "What the dude means," he said, "is you should go talk to your podner."

"Okay." James nodded, in a hurry to free his thigh from Big Top's rather personal grip. More proficiently than the first time, he got the door open.

"Don't close it," LaRue ordered.

James's chin dribbled up and down like a basketball, and he walked quickly away. LaRue watched a family of ducks paddling contentedly along the edge of the water, bobbing after cigarette filters and items unimportant to humans.

"There's no way to do this without that asshole Corelle, is there?" LaRue asked.

"Somebody's got to explain to the security company why the monitors aren't working," Monk replied, brow wrinkled in thought. "If there's no guard in the booth to call them, they'll send the police over for sure. We need a live body in that booth."

"And he already knows the plan," LaRue stated flatly.

Big Top spat out the window. He left the planning to the smart people. His buddy Monk had kept him out of trouble when they were cellmates at Atmore, and he wouldn't let him down now.

There were drumbeats in the distance. Somewhere a parade was rolling.

"Here he comes," Monk announced, scanning his mirror.

In a second James stuck his head inside the passenger window.

"I didn't do so good," he reported sadly. "Corelle wants to forget the whole thing. He's got a chance to ride in Zulu on Mardi Gras morning." James wagged his head, ready to be scolded.

"I'll try to explain the situation to him," LaRue said, and disembarked from the van. He straightened his tan polyester jacket over his sidearm, adjusted his turquoise and silver belt buckle, and walked back to the Pontiac.

Big Top stuck his head out the window to watch and started whistling a tune. Monk fixed the side mirror to keep the action in view. Outside, James kneeled down in the grass to try to find the cigarette he had dropped earlier.

They saw Rue somehow entice a fat brown-skinned man out of the car, and watched the two of them step into the shade of the tree to powwow.

It was a short conversation. Without fanfare, Rue pulled his pistol out and stuck the barrel in the vicinity of Corelle's nose. The stocky guard began to raise his plump hands in supplication, but Rue slapped them away. He patted Corelle down efficiently with his left hand, confiscated a small pistol from the man's back pants pocket, and lowered his own to Corelle's ample midriff where it might look less interesting to passing motorists or canoers on the bayou.

He escorted the big man back to the van and pointed him inside.

"What you got to say now?" Corelle grunted at James,

who held his hands out, palms up in apology, and otherwise looked helpless.

"Inside." LaRue prodded and pushed the fat man through the door.

"Put your cuffs on him," he instructed James.

"Now, now." James hesitated.

"Give me any crap," LaRue spat, "and I'll cut out your fucking tongue and feed it to the fish."

James got the point and with shaking hands quickly dug his silver handcuffs out of his pocket.

Corelle glared at his co-worker and squirmed around on the van's seat while his meaty wrists were secured behind his back.

LaRue holstered his gun and held out his hand. James gave him the key to the cuffs.

"We'll see you tomorrow at the bank at one o'clock, just as planned," LaRue told James, climbing into the van. He slammed the door home with a clang.

"Don't worry 'bout a thang," Big Top said, spitting his gum out the window.

Monk started the motor and slowly rolled the van back onto the boulevard.

"Damn," James whispered, sulking and trying not to show it. He patted his pockets for his cigarettes and lighter. "Damn," he said again.

2

Marguerite learned a lot of odd information about New Orleans on her cab ride into the city.

"See, right now you're in Jefferson Parish," her tea-skinned driver explained. His slender head, which was covered by a thin coating of enameled black hair, barely cleared the headrest. "It's the longest parish in the world, being more than two hundred miles from end to end. My name is Hossein. You may call me Hoss.

"We're crossing over Veterans Boulevard," he said. "You see all the traffic? That's because they have lotsa big Mardi Gras parades here tonight. It's a very long street."

"I thought the parades were just on Mardi Gras Day," Marguerite said, gazing at a landscape of shopping malls reminiscent of some of the more out-of-control suburbs of Chicago.

"Oh no, madam. They have parades all the time. They have even more on Mardi Gras Day. You won't be able to get around anywhere." Hossein ("call me Hoss") cut off a station wagon and ignored the blast from its horn. "And this is the

Causeway," he said, "the longest bridge in the world. It was built by Governor Huey P. Long."

"A lot of things here are the longest," she commented.

"Yes, indeed. You see these cemeteries?" Automatically Marguerite crossed herself. "It's how they bury people, on top of the ground. You got to keep the dead people in these concrete boxes or else they float away when it rains."

Really? Now that was something different. She began to think that maybe this trip would be worthwhile after all.

"And it rains a lot here, too," the cabdriver added. "Where are you from?"

"Chicago," she said.

"Now I was there a long time ago," he said, blowing his horn and changing lanes with the flip of one finger. "Back when it was a better place," he added enigmatically. "They surely have some wonderful smoked sausage up there, what they call it?"

"Kielbasa?"

"Yes, ma'am. We got a sausage like that here and everybody eats it with their red beans. You been here before?"

"No."

"You will really enjoy Mardi Gras. Everybody drink, drink, drink. It's lots of fun, if it doesn't rain, of course."

"Is it supposed to?" she asked worriedly.

"They say it might. Big storm out West. But everybody drink, drink, drink anyway. You have to watch out for the blacks though."

"What for?"

"They might steal your purse or your camera. I'm very prejudiced."

"Oh," she said.

"And they talk all this trash."

"Is it very dangerous here?"

"You must know where it's okay to go. Are you all by yourself?"

"Oh no," she lied. "I'm meeting my boyfriend."

"Okay. Well, maybe you won't have any problem." He cut across three lanes and zipped off an exit marked Claiborne Avenue. "We got to take a screwy way to get to your hotel or else we get caught in traffic."

Their route took them around the giant white oyster shell of the Superdome, which she recognized from pictures in the travel brochure.

"It's the largest stadium in the whole world," Hoss said with great satisfaction. "Now we're crossing Canal Street. You will notice how wide it is. In fact, it is the widest street in the world."

They bounced through a housing project, and Marguerite saw some black toddlers scampering over a hard-packed dirt yard chasing a blue basketball.

"Where are we?" she asked anxiously.

"This is nowhere, madam," Hoss replied carelessly, shooting across Basin Street.

"Now you are in the famous French Quarter," he exclaimed. "It is the oldest French Quarter in the world."

Old and quaint it was, the narrow streets crowded by brick structures, mortar flaking away, punctuated here and there by an iron gate that exposed a courtyard full of flowers or a hidden fountain. She had some pretty good views since the traffic had slowed to a crawl.

Hoss rolled down his window and waved frantically at the line of cars progressing fitfully ahead of them, and Marguerite understood again that it was awfully warm here. When she left Chicago there had been two feet of snow on the ground and more on the way.

As they slowly progressed, the sidewalks filled with people. They surrounded the cab, walking in the middle of the block, and getting where they wanted to go much more efficiently than she was in her taxi. The pedestrians also seemed increasingly weird—scrawny tattooed men with sleeveless black leather vests and porkpie hats, a fat couple wearing identical green jumpsuits with cameras strung on their necks, some provocative women in bright red hot pants, and clusters of loud-talking guys and gals carrying clear plastic cups of beer that sloshed as they walked.

Most of them were moving in the same direction.

"Going to the parade," Hoss explained. "I believe it must be the Iris parade, which is the longest parade in the world for nothing but women, you know. This is your hotel coming up."

The Royal Montpelier, she observed, stood in majestic splendor across the street from a burlesque show and a Takee Outee beer and fried rice emporium, and it had tall black footmen regally outfitted in red tuxedo jackets and white turbans, who sprang to life as the cab eased to the curb.

One attendant leapt into the street to open her door, blessing her with a magnificent smile.

"Welcome to the Royal Montpelier," he proclaimed, and offered his white-gloved hand.

While Hoss got her bags from the trunk and struggled to haul them to curbside, she was escorted to the grand entrance. The giant doorman raised his arm and snapped his fingers at a bellhop, a hefty man with a bristling mustache and slightly wild black hair who was stuffed into a green uniform with red epaulets and tassels on the shoulders. While the gatesman held open the gilded doors, the bellhop, with somewhat less energy than the others, collected her suitcases and led the way into the lobby.

"Checking in, ma'am? Just follow me. I'll keep an eye on your bags while you get your key."

The lobby was ornate and busy with potentially interesting male guests, but getting her room was an ordeal. A twisting line followed a pair of golden ropes, made remarkable only by the fact that most of the people in it had heaps of colorful beads piled around their necks and appeared to be inebriated. They were talking animatedly about marvelous "floats" they had seen and how you catch a rider's eye and yell, "Throw me something, mister," and how they had managed to snare this strand of silver beads or that plastic cup bearing the krewe's emblem. Word was that tonight there was an even bigger parade called "Bacchus."

Finally, Marguerite's Visa card was accepted, her keycard was slid over the counter, and she found herself in the elevator with the mountainous bellman. His brass nameplate said "Dan."

"Just here for Carnival?" he asked pleasantly.

"Yes. I've never been here before."

He asked where she was from, and she told him Chicago.

"I used to live there," he said. "Worked in a packing plant. Not much fun."

"That's why I'm here. Just to have fun."

"Do you know anyone in town?" he asked politely as the doors opened on the second floor.

"No. I wish I did have somebody to show me around."

He checked her quickly out of the corner of his eye, but evidently she didn't mean him.

"Well," he mumbled, "just take a walk outside. There's a whole street full of people out there who would be glad to show you things you might not see in Illinois. For starters, you also might try the bar on the roof."

3

Edward and Wendell thought they might have to walk all the way to town from the airport, the highway was so crowded. This was their first trip together away from Atlanta, where Edward was a stockbroker and Wendell was one of 193 vice presidents of a rapidly expanding regional bank. His specialty was accounts receivable financing, which, he had learned, would stop a conversation at any party. They had picked Mardi Gras in New Orleans as their great getaway—a week of wearing masks, getting lost in the crowd, and holing up together in a Vieux Carré guest house a good friend had recommended as "private and cozy."

"It's just a matter of getting there," Edward mused encouragingly. They nestled like new potatoes in one of the back seats of a ten-passenger shuttle bus carrying a full load of uncomfortable airport travelers.

The driver answered a couple of questions about the meaning of Mardi Gras and how many people came to New Orleans at this time of the year, and then he ran out of things to say and just grumbled about all the bad drivers in all the cars with Mississippi and Texas tags.

And when they finally exited the interstate, it seemed that their hotel was the last one on the route. First they had to stop at the Columns, the Claiborne Mansion, Le Pavillon, Comfort Suites, the Econo Lodge, the Château Sonesta, the Holiday Inn, the Royal Montpelier, and the Maison De Ville. When the driver finally threw the gearshift into park, barked "Lafitte's Lair," and jumped out of his seat, they had been nearly two hours in the van and were crying out for pain relief.

"I must have wine," Wendell gasped desperately.

"Surely there's a store around here," Edward said, but looking through the limo's dusty safety glass, it was clear that Lafitte's Lair was not the run-of-the-mill elegantly restored bed-and-breakfast that one might find, say, in Savannah or Charleston. There were, in fact, no signs that the establishment had been restored at all. The outside walls were cracked and soiled—quaint, to be sure, but unmistakably deteriorating—and the sidewalk was loaded with bits of food and empty plastic cups. One spilled out a pasty purple liquid when Edward misstepped.

"I fear that sports fans are near," Wendell said ominously.

Pigeons had taken charge of the litter and were strutting around importantly.

What might be the front door was a boarded-up archway, painted black, with a doorbell and a peephole in the middle. They would not immediately have recognized this as the way one entered had not the limo driver hurried in that direction with their bags. There was, however, a tastefully small painted sign off to the side of the door, bolted to the age-softened brick, with the words "Lafitte's Lair" on it.

"I guess this is the right place," Edward said doubtfully.

"Home at last," Wendell replied weakly. He twitched his nose, trying to decipher the warm richly odored air, while Edward tipped the driver heavily. They watched him putter away.

Wendell bravely rang the bell.

They stood patiently for a minute or two, assimilating their new, somewhat mildewed surroundings, and then Edward tried the latch. The door creaked open.

Tentatively, they stepped into a cool, backlit grotto. It was a tiny office partitioned by a polished oak counter on which lay a pile of tourist brochures and an open leather guest book. There was also a credit card machine. The space was surprisingly neat and clean and suggested more luxury than the shuttered exterior.

Finding no one in attendance, Edward tinkled the silver bell on the counter. After a moment, from the beaded curtain behind, a slender figure entered, dressed in a plum leather vest and tight black pants and looking remarkably feline. She had straight black hair, and had chosen glossy black lipstick. There were silver bracelets on her wrists. Her voice had an accent they couldn't place, but which seemed somehow incongruous with her appearance. A local resident might have recognized it as Chalmette.

"How may I help you?" she asked.

"Edward Doyle. Wendell Rappold. Reservations for the week," Edward said.

"Now where is that book," the woman, apparently the person in charge, said. She rummaged about under the counter. "I'm just sort of filling in for the owner of the place while he's out. Which could be a long time. Okay," she said, and came up with a lacquered clipboard.

With obvious amazement she said, "I see your names right here. There's a note too. Let me see if I can read it." She turned the board sideways. "Want street view. Want privacy," she read slowly. She put a finger to her lips. Her nails were enameled black. "I guess I'll put you in the annex." She winked.

"Is that good?" Wendell asked.

"I would like it." She smiled and found a key.

"Follow me," she said, floating around the counter. She stepped through the archway to the hot street outside. She led them around the corner and down the block, to three granite steps ascending to a tall green shuttered doorway.

"Nobody knows how big this place is," she explained as she worked her key into the old Yale lock. "I think Sidney truthfully owns the whole block. Lots of freaks live on this street. Lots of 'em," she added to herself. She threw the green shutters aside and stepped in.

She couldn't find a light switch but knew where some long pink candles were kept.

The two visitors, enthralled by the sense of having fallen through the looking glass, waited at the edge of the sunlight while she got the candles lit. Carefully, she placed one in a saucer on the dining room table and the other on the floor by a fat stuffed sofa in the living room.

"Come on in," she urged. "I've already found you three bottles of wine."

Oil paintings of old men in muttonchop whiskers came

alive in the glow. A comfortable couch, a tall ceiling, narrow shafts of daylight entering horizontally through the slits in the shutters closed over the windows, slowly emerged from the darkness.

"Isn't it nice?" she asked. "I'm looking for light bulbs."

She found some in a cupboard.

"Don't you want to imprint my card?" Edward, very honest, asked.

"Maybe I should," she said, as if the thought of payment had just struck her. "Want to give it to me?"

"I guess." Edward located his wallet and handed the green plastic over to her.

"I'll leave it up front for Sidney," she said, and drifted outside.

By candlelight, Edward and Wendell began poking about their new digs. Edward, mystified about how he had lost possession of his American Express card, stumbled upon a yellowing issue of a magazine called *Gambit* that had a map of Lee Harvey Oswald landmarks. Wendell discovered the Merlot.

"I like this place," Edward said, tossing the magazine aside.

"Do you think they know we're here?" Wendell asked, seeking a corkscrew.

"I wonder if she'll bring back my card."

"Shall I close the door?"

"Never mind." Edward uncorked the bottle he was handed and dropped the lead foil to the floor. He moved into the sunlight washing through the doorway, leaned against the wall, and sighed. "Let's just let it happen."

4

Tubby's favorite part of Mardi Gras was Thoth. If what you wanted to do was crash into people, drink beer, eat fried chicken, and hop around for rubber monkeys, almost any parade would do. Over the past twenty-five or thirty years, he supposed, he had made a fool of himself at the feet of every king, duke, knight, maid, and big shot in the Carnival Kingdom, sometimes with a screaming child on each shoulder and sometimes with nobody but himself to blame. He had carted home wheelbarrows full of trinkets and couldn't tell you where any of them were today. He had shouted himself hoarse, stared awestruck at teenage bosoms, and swiped bouncing cups from the grasp of babes. Of Mardi Gras, he had seen it all. What he liked best was Thoth.

It was a nice old parade that rolled slowly through the neighborhood he lived in on the Sunday morning before Mardi Gras. It followed a circuitous route past the numerous old folks' homes and hospitals that dotted the area. The theme was cheering up the shut-ins. If you picked a location near a platoon of old gray-haired gents or ladies in wheelchairs, you were certain to get clobbered with beads. There

27

were also some convents along the way, and the nuns who came out on the sidewalk in their habits got tons of good stuff, too.

Since the krewe rode uptown in the daylight, there were hordes of children out for the event. As far as some of the little kids knew, this was Mardi Gras. Their parents never ventured out of doors on Fat Tuesday itself because, hell, nowadays you could watch the whole thing on television. And when you wanted a cold beer and a ham sandwich, or needed to use the bathroom, hey, no problem.

Lots of people Tubby knew held Thoth parties. Usually they would open their homes or backyards an hour before the parade. They would set out the tiny muffalettas, or the roast beef, or light that crawfish pot and start mixing Bloody Marys right after they fed the kids breakfast. Then all the little boys and girls could run around like maniacs, painting their faces and spreading rumors about when the parade would pass, while their parents and grandparents enjoyed the sunshine outside and carried on the city's oldest tradition.

Since his divorce from Mattie, Tubby had noticed with interest and some regret how their once common friends had dealt with party invitations. Mainly, he did not get as many. First to abandon him were several high-class attorneys who lived in the immediate environs of his old house on State Street. They had correctly understood that it was Mattie Dubonnet who was the more scintillating around the grillades and grits and that Tubby, though undeniably a lawyer, kept a fishing boat in his driveway. He did not truly view them as companions.

Tubby had, however, kept the cream of the crop in his opinion. Such as Jerry Molideau, the financial adviser, who lived on Chestnut with his girlfriend, Bonita. She was good enough to send Tubby an invitation to their annual pre-Thoth celebration addressed by hand to "Tubby Dubonnet and Guest."

Collette, his youngest daughter, had agreed to join him for the occasion. She still lived at home with her mother. On the phone she offered to meet her father at Magazine and Jefferson, right where the parade passed and in the thick of the crowd. Knowing her proclivity for diversion, he said he would pick her up instead and they would walk together down State Street. Okay, they made a deal.

So now he found himself by the curb outside the house where he and Mattie had raised a family, and he was wondering if she would ever paint the porch. He had mowed around the trees and azaleas in this front yard so many times he could probably do it in his sleep, and he had to admit he missed it. But did he miss Mattie, who still called herself Dubonnet? Not on your life.

"Well, hello, Tubby," she said when she answered the bell. She gave him a big smile. A discreet golden favor from an old Comus ball adorned her perennially tanned, attractive, and not forgotten chest. The rest of her was stylishly draped in a white, fairylike beach dress.

He grinned in admiration and shook his head, and was glad he was wearing sunglasses so she couldn't see his eyes.

"You're looking good," he said honestly.

"Are we ready to go?" Collette brushed past her mother.

At fifteen, she was a smaller version of the original, just developing some pretty significant curves. Until the last year she had been real smart in school. Now, like her mother, she was starting to expect to be the center of attention in any crowd larger than three and was generally getting to be a know-it-all. Unlike her mother, she still loved Tubby.

"Ready and waiting," he said.

"Then let's head out." Collette took her father's elbow, turned him around, and hustled him down the walk to the gate that was about to fall off its hinges.

"I'll be at the Ormonds'," Mattie called, to let Tubby know she was still in demand. Poinsette Ormond was among the high-class attorneys he was personally glad to be rid of. "Maybe I'll see y'all at the parade."

Tubby was halfway down the block before he let his stomach out. Brief encounters with the ex-wife were always nerve-racking.

"Are you in a hurry to get to the parade?" he asked Collette, who was prodding him on ahead.

"No, I'm just glad to get out of the house," she said in exasperation.

"What's wrong?" he asked, trying to match her stride down the oak-lined sidewalk, sections of which had been broken and lifted by the trees' massive roots. They were passing lovely homes and tended hedges, all belonging to his former neighbors.

"You know how Mattie is. She just keeps asking questions. Who I'm talking to on the telephone. Why Brenda is dropping out of school. Just bugging me all the time."

"You call your mother Mattie?"

"When she's like that, I do. She's absolutely convinced I'm going to start doing drugs and pierce my nose and go grunge."

These were exactly Tubby's fears.

"Ha ha," he laughed.

"Really," she said in agreement. She waved at some boys in ragged blue jeans and baseball caps sitting on the wide steps between the columns of a grand old wooden porch.

"So you don't like nose rings?" he asked.

"They may look fine on somebody eighteen, but not on a girl my age," she said sensibly.

His brow furrowed.

"Will we have to stay long at the Molideaus'? What are you supposed to call them? They're not married, are they?"

"Her last name is Gayoso. Just call him Mr. Molideau and her Ms. Gayoso. We'll stay awhile and get something to eat and then go to the parade. We can go back to their house whenever we want and use the bathroom."

"Why don't they get married? Haven't they been together for years and years?"

"I have no idea," Tubby said. "They own the house together. I guess they just have their own jobs and want to keep their lives a little bit separate."

"I think that's so cool."

He did not have a chance to find out what part of the

arrangement she found cool, because they reached the gate of the Molideau yard.

"Howdy, stranger," called Bonita, in yellow shorts and a Crescent City Classic T-shirt. "Is this Collette? Honey, you've grown!"

Collette got through the introductions without a hitch, and it did not take her long to find the teenagers she knew, who had isolated themselves in a distant corner of the yard. Having been abandoned by his escort, Tubby joined the men standing around the pirogue full of ice and Langenstein's Lager.

"Make way for lawyer Dubonnet." Jerry, hale and hearty with beer foam on his upper lip, pressed a wet bottle into Tubby's fist.

"Happy Mardi Gras, son," he said. "Let's get this day going right."

Tubby inhaled deeply the peppery vapors of crawfish steaming and took a long cool swallow. It looked like they even had an entire turkey frying in one of those pots. A child darted in for a handful of ice, and somewhere a clock chimed eleven.

"I saw you on the *Angela* show," somebody said to Tubby. "You were talking about some scam a drug company was running over at the Moskowitz Labs. Or was it a murder?"

"It was a murder," Tubby said, accepting a fried oyster from a towheaded six-year-old in charge of a full tray.

"Yeah, it was a very interesting program."

"I tell you what, Angela's really great," Tubby said.

"She always has on them earrings."

"Yeah. I thought she was real nice-looking."

"Didn't I see you come in here with some babe?"

"Uh, that was my daughter."

"Oh. Have another beer."

And where could she have gotten to? Tubby wondered, looking around.

An old man named Russell Ligi was getting more and more nervous, which made him more and more angry, the longer he had to wait at the Algiers ferry landing. He was sitting in his car with his door open, feet planted on the iron ramp, furiously puffing a Swisher Sweet. A seagull landed beside him, and he kicked at it. His instructions had been to take the eleven o'clock boat and someone would contact him. The ferry was late, of course. He had been watching it piss around on the far side of the river for half an hour. He desperately needed to use the can.

The boat finally chugged up and discharged its load, and a punk in an orange vest waved him aboard. By then, Ligi was ready to pop off at anyone who volunteered. A dozen other vehicles rumbled onto the ferry behind him, and they were all crammed together in three tight rows on the open deck.

As soon as he could shut his engine off Ligi was out of the car. He leaned on the rail and crushed the butt of his cigar into the sheet metal deck with his heel. Sunlight broke through the overcast sky for a moment, causing the river to sparkle wildly. He had to squint to see the face of the large, square-jawed man who had appeared on the railing beside him.

"Ligi?" the man asked.

"Yeah, sure!"

"C'mon, let's get in my car."

The big man turned away without waiting for a reply and led Ligi to a mustard-colored Cadillac parked farther back in the jam. Ligi hopped from foot to foot while the man worked the locks. He got in and slammed the door.

"So? What?" Ligi had out another of his Sweets and tapped it on the dashboard.

The stranger, with curly blond hair worn long to cover a few sparse patches, stared at Ligi until the old man stopped fidgeting.

"Mr. Ligi, the deal is all set. That's what I'm supposed to tell you. The sale is going ahead. I've got the papers right here for you to sign."

"Sign? Right now? What about the fucking letter I told them about? You got that?"

"We're getting it. It will all be taken care of."

"You got old Parvelle to give it up? What's that old thief getting out of this?"

"That's not your affair. You made your deal, and the deal is going down on Mardi Gras."

"You got to be fucking joking," Ligi sputtered. "When do I get paid? Why am I signing now in the front seat of a car on a goddamn ferryboat? Where's my money?"

"You're going to get it later this week," the man explained patiently. "Right after Mardi Gras."

"This is bullshit, sonny. That's what the chickees say when they're trying to talk some guy into marrying them. After that it's, 'I'm tired, honey. Oh, I'm so tired.' Nobody does business like that."

"Mr. Ligi, I was asked to treat you with respect, considering your age, but if you don't stop breathing in my face I'm going to smash your fucking head up against that windshield. So listen up."

Taken aback, Ligi clamped his jaw shut.

"The thing is, you sign your deed now. You forget about that letter, like it doesn't exist. When the investors finish the transaction, which should be in a couple of days, you will get your money. I'll deliver it personally."

"And I'm just supposed to trust you?" Ligi shook his head violently.

The big man's hand shot out and grabbed Ligi's nose, fixing it in place. Deliberately, he squeezed and twisted slowly one way, then the other, causing Ligi to squirm and stomp his feet on the carpet.

"Ow, ow, ow," he yelped.

"Mr. Ligi," the man said, holding him tight, "this ferry is about to dock, and before it does you're going to sign the documents I brought with me. Then you can go on about your business."

Mopping the blood off his upper lip with his handkerchief, Ligi signed his name on the sheets of paper as they were pushed in front of him.

"These are supposed to be notarized," he complained.

"We got a notary." The stranger folded the papers and put them in his pocket. "You better get back in your car," he said pleasantly. "We're there."

• • •

With sirens whooping and street cleaners gobbling debris and hosing down the pavement, the Thoth parade faded away down Magazine Street. That was it for Tubby.

Walking home after the parade, both weighted down with many, many beads, Collette invited her father to rendezvous with her crowd on Mardi Gras. So-and-so was parking a truck at the corner of Third Street and St. Charles, and they would have an ice chest, and everybody could come there and watch Rex and all the trucks. Her sisters, Debbie and Christine, would probably spend part of the day there.

Maybe, he said, but the idea of staying home, hanging out in the backyard, and listening to the beat of distant drums had a lot of appeal, too.

"They're going to bring a grill and barbecue stuff all day," she said, which made the invitation a lot more tempting. "They're going to cook hamburgers and sausage and roast some oysters on the grill." Perhaps he would take a stroll down there after all, if the weather was nice. The forecast, however, said possible showers.

"It can't rain on Mardi Gras." Collette was certain of that.

"If it does, you'll just have to think of all the fun we had today."

"Right, Daddy," she said, and kissed his cheek.

Opening the wobbly gate, she ran up the walk and waved from the front steps.

Replaying her parting smile in his mind, Tubby set off on

foot toward the house, a smaller one, that was his new home.

It was about six blocks away—close enough if somebody needed him. It was on a nice street with nice lawns and mostly nice people. Some, you could tell, were a little better off than he was. That thought got him thinking about his money problems. Only a few months ago he had lucked into a small fortune, but, characteristically, he had blown it. Sigh. Specifically, he had let himself be talked into buying Mike's Bar. It was a great place to hang out with the right sort of people, and he could get all the booze he wanted wholesale, but it didn't turn a profit. Meanwhile, his law practice was suffering from inattention, and he had lost a few bucks at the track. His bills, tuition and child support for three daughters, were not going away, that was a fact. And now his oldest daughter, Debbie, was getting married and naturally expected him to pay for the wedding. His suggestion that she elope had been ignored. Tubby unlocked the front door of his house and walked straight through to the kitchen for a beer.

But, you know, all that was not what was really bothering him. He had long ago realized that worrying about money was just a big waste of time, just an excuse to keep from thinking about significant things. He preferred to avoid thinking about those, of course. But, facing facts, his real trouble was—he was lonesome.

The kids were gone and his wife was ancient history. He did not even like to dwell upon Jynx Margolis, his well-heeled consort at parties. She could be fairly amorous, if it suited her schedule, but there really wasn't any fire there. He badly needed a better class of companion.

Tubby glanced at the wall clock and was startled to see that it was four o'clock. How could a morning parade last so long?

He sat at the kitchen table and idly leafed through the sports section of the *Times-Picayune.* He had already read it while drinking coffee this morning, so he lost interest quickly. He tossed it on the chair and stared at the stove, a lawyer home alone. "Now what?" he said out loud.

An hour later he was holding down a stool at Mike's Bar, sipping an old-fashioned. Larry, somewhat opaque in the dusty light behind the bar, fixed Tubby's drink extra strong, with an older brand of bourbon than his undiscriminating customers got and a double shot of Isle of Capri cherry juice. Larry basically ran the place now. He had tended its bar for thirty years—the whole time Mr. Mike owned the joint—and he had taken on the tavern's coloration. Tubby pretty much left him alone.

"Nobody's playing cards tonight," Tubby observed, tipping his head toward the round table in the corner. It was empty of its usual circle of gamblers.

"They'll be in later," Larry said. "The judge already called in to see who was here." He meant Judge Duzet, who spent his evenings at Mike's and was facing mandatory retirement this year.

"When's he comin' in, darlin'?" Mrs. Pearl called from down the bar. She was a busty widow of advancing years with a stiff ball of pink hair. Mr. Pearl had blown up in a grain elevator and left her a little pension.

"He said after a while," Larry reported, and drifted away to wash a glass.

"You all by yourself tonight, sweetheart?" Mrs. Pearl asked Tubby.

"Yeah." He kicked back his drink and grimaced.

"Well, I'll join you." She hefted her thighs off her stool and walked over to climb up beside Tubby. "Watch my purse, Larry," she called. She didn't have to worry. The only other guy in the place was asleep in the corner, a bottle of Budweiser by his elbow. Tubby hoped things would pick up later.

"You been to any parades?" she asked, straightening her dress beneath her.

"Yeah, I went to Thoth today with my daughter."

"Oh, that's a nice parade. I didn't go this year because my son's in the hospital."

"I'm sorry to hear that. What's wrong with him?"

"He's got an ulcer."

"Really? How old is he?"

"If I told you that, you'd know how old I am," Mrs. Pearl said slyly, and winked one of her long black lashes.

"I'd guess you might be pushing thirty," Tubby said.

"Oh, my my. You'd better have another drink." She patted Tubby's knee.

Larry buzzed in two of the lady's friends, Newt and Vincent Blando. They were twins who lived together and went to the same church as Mrs. Pearl, just a block away.

They stood around and gossiped, and Newt said let's play

cards. The barkeep sold them a fresh deck of Squeezers, and they carried their drinks back to the big table. The drunk at the bar woke up and spilled his beer.

With an air of regret, Mrs. Pearl uprooted herself again.

"Want to play with us, dear?" she asked.

"Not tonight," Tubby said. "My daughter's getting married and I've got to save my money."

"Oh, I love weddings," Mrs. Pearl said. "Be sure to invite me."

"Okay." He probably would.

"Want another one?" Larry asked.

"I don't think I could stand the excitement," Tubby muttered. "Where's all the action tonight?"

"It ain't here," Larry said.

5

Monk, Big Top, and LaRue drove to the Night's Rite Motel on Chef Menteur Highway. They wanted two rooms with two double beds apiece, adjoining, since their party now included a fourth member, security man Corelle. He was currently gagged and cuffed, wrist to ankle, and wedged in the back of the van between the generator and the box of tools.

The motel manager was a portly Pakistani with long raven sideburns. He had a pot of bulgur steaming on the stove in his apartment behind the office, and he was tending it by himself since his wife had gone off to Schwegmann's to buy some red peppers. He took LaRue's cash but also insisted on a credit card. LaRue gave him a stolen one. Satisfied with that, the manager handed over two keys on green tags.

"Want more ice, come back here," he said, filling up a plastic bucket from a machine behind the desk that was leaking darkly on the stained blue carpet.

"Where's a good place to eat around here?" LaRue asked.

"Tastee Donuts next door, or, you know, Domino delivers." The manager thought he could smell his dinner burning and excused himself.

LaRue grunted and pocketed the keys.

He walked back to the van.

"Room one-oh-nine," he told Monk. "Find a spot right in front if you can."

I hope the room smells better than the office, Rue thought sourly as he crossed the parking lot. It was like a Chinese restaurant in there. He noticed, however, that the outdoor air carried the unmistakable aroma of coffee, and he figured that must be coming from the donut shop.

"What do you want us to do with the dummy?" Monk asked LaRue when they had parked and stepped out of the minivan. The big-eared Texan with the spooky eyes had taken Corelle prisoner; it was his job to decide where to stick him.

"He'll stay in the room with me. Unlock the back of the van and help me get him."

Corelle was packed horizontally, and his eyes blinked open as soon as the hatch lid flipped up. He was sweating profusely, and his thick lips twitched around the handkerchief pulled through his teeth. He let out a long growl.

"I'm going to untie the gag. If you make any noise I'm going to put it back on and kick you in the nuts," LaRue said simply. "Understand?"

Corelle rumbled and managed a small nod.

LaRue pushed the heavy body around on the floor of the van until he could reach the knot with ease. With a few rough jerks he got it loose.

Corelle gasped and swallowed deeply.

LaRue unlocked the cuffs and got his captive into a sitting position. He helped him get out of the van. Corelle stood up unsteadily, shaking his head, and put a hand on the open hatchback for support.

"Come along," LaRue instructed, and directed Corelle by the elbow into the little motel room. Big Top and Monk followed to see what the plan was. Big Top checked himself in the mirror on the plastic dresser and whipped out a comb to fix his hair.

"Hey, man, let's talk about this," Corelle said, looking around hopefully and massaging his biceps.

"Later," LaRue said, and startled everyone by spinning the guard around and shoving him face forward onto the bed. He was on top of the man before he could react and, pinning him with a knee stuck painfully into the guard's back, fastened the handcuffs back on his wrists. He pulled the handkerchief out of his pocket and yanked it tight around Corelle's mouth again, making his scream of protest unintelligible. He flipped both sides of the quilted polyester bedspread over the prostrate victim and wrapped him up like a tamale.

"Help me get him in the closet," he ordered Monk and Big Top. They exchanged worried glances, but each quickly grabbed a piece of the body.

"Ain't you afraid he'll smother in there?" Big Top asked.

"Fuck him," LaRue said.

Clumsily, they worked the squirming carcass into a semi-upright position in the closet beside the bathroom and stood back to look.

"Make a commotion," LaRue told the bedspread, "and I'll set you on fire. I'm a bad dude." He closed the door.

"You guys got any booze in the van?" LaRue asked.

"I'll get it," Big Top said, hurrying out of the room. Happy hour had arrived.

Tubby went home early. He dozed off in the living room while Hoda Kotb read the ten o'clock news on television. He was dreaming about spending money during a rerun of *The Price Is Right* when the telephone woke him up.

He grabbed it before realizing he didn't want to talk to anybody. Too late, he had already said hello.

"Hey, Tubby, it's me, Dan."

Dan was an old pal, working these days as a bellhop at a hotel downtown. They went way back to those good ol' college days best forgotten, when they had filled up the top two weight classes on the wrestling team. The bigger guy had been known as "Red" Dan because he would organize a demonstration against any hint of bourgeois injustice on campus. He had, for example, thumbtacked a manifesto on the athletic department's door calling for student rebellion because the school jerked the basketball scholarship of a fraternal troublemaker, but only after the team's winning season was safely in the bag. All of the jocks threatened to strike, but then they forgot about it and the school kicked the kid out anyway.

"Whaddya say, Dan?" Tubby came awake.

"I think I got a client for you."

"Really?" Tubby said warily.

"Don't sound too thrilled. Am I interrupting something?"

"No, that's okay. I'm just watching the tube." His lack of

excitement was because Dan had finally found his true vocation in life as a roving union organizer for the Industrial Workers of the World. He blew through town infrequently but never quietly. The kind of clients he sent to Tubby all had hopeless cases, no money, eviction notices stuck to their door, and five hungry kids at home.

"Yeah," Dan said excitedly, "there's this lady staying at the hotel, and me and her got to talking a little bit. She's from, like Iowa, and doesn't know krewes from cornflakes, know what I mean? Not too streetwise."

"Yeah."

"So, the time-share cultists got her. They kidnapped her on Bourbon Street, took her down to Elysian Fields, made her watch their mind control films, and sold her a time-share she doesn't want."

"Has she paid for it?"

"Yeah, like fifteen thousand. And look, it's for a week in August."

"Wow." Tubby laughed. "Why did she do that?"

"They said it was the week of the Belle Chasse Blessing of the Lowquats Festival, or something like that. She's confused. She wants out of the deal. She wants a lawyer."

This was a pleasant surprise. If she could write a check for $15,000 and get a room at the Royal Montpelier, she ought to be able to pay Tubby. And if he moved quickly it should be a cinch to get her dough back because there was a special provision in the law, he knew, for the protection of corn-fed midwesterners who bought time-shares and then repented.

"Okay, I'll talk to her." Tubby reached for his pen.

"Want to come down tonight? We can catch a few brews when I get off work."

"No way, bro. I've been parading all day with Collette. I need my beauty sleep."

"Too bad. The Quarter is absolutely hopping. There's a great sax man playing at O'Mulberry's Irish Bar. Of course, they might pass the hat for the IRA."

"What? No, I can't do it."

"Okay, well look—how about tomorrow?"

"Yeah. Tell her to come to my office. I've got a couple of errands to run in the morning. Say, two o'clock."

"She'll be there, man."

"You sure?"

"Absolutely!" Dan exclaimed. "She's put her fate in my hands. I told her about the time I worked for John Deere tractors. She thinks I'm the only upright dude in New Orleans."

"Did you tell her you left the lug nuts off the inside tires?"

"That didn't come up in our conversation. Hey, looks like I got to get back to work. We got people pouring in here from all over the world, man."

"Have fun."

"Don't forget, I'm referring this lady to you because I like her, and I know you'll play straight with her."

"Okay, Dan. Have a good Mardi Gras."

"I'm raking in the dough, buddy. Workers of the world, unite."

He hung up, and Tubby went into the kitchen to look for something to drink that might clear his head.

6

Willie LaRue slept a peaceful sleep and came wide awake, with the covers tucked neatly under his chin, at seven o'clock when the first sunlight came through the crack in the curtains. He never had trouble sleeping, and he never remembered his dreams. Long ago, when his father was kicking the shit out of him because he couldn't learn to throw a lariat around a fence post in the backyard, a skill damn important to his old man, LaRue had learned to turn his mind off and on. When it was off he felt no pain. When it was on he could burn a hole through your head, he was so focused.

This morning, he was focused on how to rob a bank. His prisoner, Corelle, was still wrapped in the bedspread and stuffed in the closet. He had passed out quietly in the middle of the night. Assuming he was alive, Corelle remained a part of the plan.

LaRue brushed his teeth and knocked back three 500mg vitamin C tablets, his own private tonic for staying alert. He would need any edge he could get to carry off the job, especially with the two morons from Mississippi, as he had tagged

Big Top and Monk. He had begun to believe they were queer for each other. Prison will do that to you, as LaRue well knew. He took a shower and carefully washed himself.

He was dressed and had dragged the mummy out of the closet into the center of the room, when there was a knock on the door.

"It's me." It was Big Top's high-pitched voice.

LaRue stepped over Corelle and took the chain off the door. Big Top came in bearing a cardboard tray of coffee from Tastee Donuts.

"Morning," he said, and stopped when he saw the pile on the floor.

"Is he all right?" Big Top did not really care. He was just curious how bad a dude Rue really was.

"Don't know yet," LaRue said. He took off the plastic lid and tasted his coffee. Unimpressed, he set it down on top of the Formica dresser.

"Let's unwrap him," he said.

They had to roll the body around on the rug to get the bedspread off him. Corelle was alive enough to groan deliriously. There was a stain, blood or vomit, on the rag in his mouth, and his eyelids were wet with tears.

"We're gonna bring you back to life, big fellow," LaRue said, pinching his earlobe. "Yes, sir, we are."

Fifteen minutes later, after administering a combination of cold water and hard slaps, they had the guard sitting unassisted in a chair. He was wagging his head from side to side and moaning softly, not yet ready to speak.

Monk had joined them, and they were all drinking their coffee and watching the *Today* show with Katie Couric. Big Top had a Hubig's peach pie in his freckled hand, and he was dropping crumbs of sugar on the rug. The topic of the show was a serial killer who had buried bodies in public places all over Oklahoma. People had apparently seen him digging holes with a pick and shovel on numerous occasions, but nobody had ever questioned him or noticed that he was planting people. Or if they had noticed, nobody had thought it was worth reporting to anyone who might care more.

LaRue laughed soundlessly.

"Do you believe these people seen what he was doin' and didn't say nothing?" Big Top exclaimed.

"You just gotta do things in broad daylight," Monk said. "That's when nobody sees a thing." Monk had once robbed a used-car lot in Talladega in broad daylight and been apprehended by the Alabama State Police in about twenty minutes, but he had forgotten that.

"Which is just what we're doing when we go into the bank today." Big Top swallowed the last of his pie. "We'll just roll in our box of tools like we're the King of Spain and nobody will say a thing."

"That's right," LaRue said, thinking that Big Top could have been a stand-in for Howdy Doody if he'd had the brains. He prodded the slowly reviving guard with the toe of his lizard skin cowboy boot.

"And you're going to walk right in with us, aren't you, soldier?"

Corelle licked his lips. He wasn't able to communicate just yet.

The big guard was feeling better after an air-conditioned ride downtown in the Astro van. Somewhere in the maze of tall buildings Monk found a space in a freight zone. He pointed out the "Closed for Mardi Gras" sign on the watchmaker's shop they were in front of. Half a block away was the main entrance of the First Alluvial Bank building. With Big Top's help Monk lifted the heavy generator and the tool chest out of the hatchback and placed them carefully on the sidewalk. A light rain was falling. With Corelle and LaRue joined at the elbow and bringing up the rear, they rolled the equipment down the block at a fast clip. All three robbers wore white jumpsuits over their clothes with "Stanley Sanitation" stenciled in red thread on their breast pockets. This had been LaRue's idea, and Monk had lifted them from a laundry truck in Hattiesburg.

It was shortly after noon, and bankers, anxious to get out of downtown before the day's first wave of parades hit, were streaming out of the building. A petite black woman was standing on the steps talking to a fat man in a navy-blue suit. "Have you got any big plans for Carnival, Tania?" LaRue heard the man ask. "Pastor Green and I expect to practice our singing at the church," she replied sweetly. "We're not much on parties." LaRue held one of the large glass doors open and asked the citizens to stand aside while, grunting and groaning, Monk and Big Top manipulated the bulky items through. Corelle followed, looking dejectedly at the slowly rotating security camera mounted high on the wall.

They had to pass through an elevator lobby. At its far end, on the left-hand side, were the tall marble portals by which one entered the vast cathedral of the banking lobby. On the right, down wide stone steps, was the vault and the room full of safe-deposit boxes. A small elevator also descended to the basement, for the use of the men from Wells Fargo who picked up sacks of coins and currency, wheelchair-bound customers, and LaRue's crew.

LaRue got his men aboard and got Corelle's attention with a jerk of his thumb. Grudgingly, the guard joined them in the small box. His compliance, at least temporarily, had been assured after LaRue went through his wallet, extracted a color photograph of two grinning boys, and promised to sell them into slavery in Mexico if Corelle did not go with the program. He also reminded Corelle that, despite spending the night wrapped in a blanket, his portion of the take was still $50,000. That part was bullshit, of course.

When the elevator opened in the basement, its passengers were facing a glass-encased booth in which the worried face of James could plainly be seen fluttering around inside. He waved them forward and unlocked his cubicle to join them.

"I'm sure glad you're with us," he said warmly to Corelle, who frowned at him.

"Is everything okay?" James asked.

"Everything's just fine, though our generator got wet

bringing it in," LaRue said. "What's with the security camera upstairs in the lobby?"

"Them and this one here"—James indicated the little black box behind the robbers on top of the elevator door—"display on my monitors in the booth and also back at the company. I turned 'em all off, like I told you I would, right at twelve forty-five. I'm gonna call the company now and tell 'em it's just a short. They're always shorting out or busting a fuse for some reason. They only get worried if they don't hear from me in maybe twenty or thirty minutes."

"So, call them now," LaRue instructed.

"Right," James said. "I'll call them." He trotted back into the booth and picked up a red phone.

Off to the left of the guard booth the massive round door of the vault filled the wall. It was built of gunmetal-gray steel and was at least ten feet in diameter. It was properly outfitted in shiny brass wheels and fancy rods and gave the impression of absolute impenetrability. Everybody looked it over with interest, but the safe unfortunately was not their target. Only LaRue knew what that was. All Monk and Big Top were after was money.

Their mission, for the next twelve or fourteen hours, lay at the other end of the hall. Past a walnut desk and a pair of light pink embroidered chairs was a marble-floored room containing the 1,200 safe-deposit boxes of the First Alluvial Bank.

James jabbered a few syllables into the red phone, which was all that was needed to allay the concerns of the spacey technonerds at SecureGuard headquarters. The array of equipment the company had installed at Alluvial Bank was notoriously prone to inexplicable shorts and blowouts. They gratefully accepted James's opinion that the problem was the wiring at the bank.

When this fine institution was erected soon after the Great War, it had been the tallest building for a long ways, the Port of New Orleans handled every banana eaten in America, and the science of electrical service was in its infancy. Hidden behind the building's repeatedly thickened walls were tapestries of circuits, computer wire, and telephone cables, and even miles of copper strands on porcelain spools left over from the birth of the Industrial Revolution that might or might not still do something. It was a wonder the lights came on. Rogue security cameras were routine.

James could still control these cameras, however, and they responded to his touch. With a flip of his dexterous brown fingers, he restored to view, on his monitors, the upstairs lobby and the sidewalk outside the bank. He left blank the cameras on his booth and in the safe-deposit room. Humming as he worked, he checked out the world above and said, "Ain't hardly anyone left in the building now, and the bank's closed up tight."

"Shoo'ee, look at that rain outside," Big Top said from over his shoulder.

"Weather like this they ain't gonna be no question about these cameras shorting out," James said.

"Long as we got juice for the generator everything is A-okay, right, Thelonious?" LaRue poked Monk in the stomach. "Now let's get it fired up and go to work."

• • •

Collette's day before Mardi Gras had begun on a high note. Her mother had screamed up the steps to wake her a little after ten o'clock, it being a "teacher workday" and a student day off, to ask her if she wanted to speak to her friend Norene on the phone. Of course she did, and Norene had invited her to a pool party at her house on Versailles Boulevard. Norene said there might actually not be any swimming because her dad hadn't cleaned the water since November and, being around 85 degrees, it was probably too cool by local standards anyway. But they would sit by the pool and maybe play some board games. Boys with beer were expected. Her parents were gone to Disney World with her younger brothers. Everything was going to be *très* phat. Please, please come.

Putting together a clean outfit and navigating past Mom were the only major problems. She had to run a load through the washing machine while she ate her strawberry yogurt, and to smooth the way, she also agreed to wash a load of her mother's with only a token complaint.

"Don't forget bleach," her mother cautioned.

"Obviously," Collette said. "I'm going over to Norene's this afternoon."

"What's she doing?"

"Nothing. She's lonely since her parents went to Disney World. She just wants company. We'll probably go to a show."

"Okay. You'll be home for dinner?" Mattie lit a cigarette.

"We might get something to eat afterwards."

"Just let me know. When you do my shorts, please take

them out of the dryer after just a minute or two, or I'll never get the wrinkles out."

"I know."

"Thank you."

Problem solved.

7

Tubby was stepping out of the shower, feeling groggy, when he heard his front doorbell ring. He threw on his bathrobe and padded downstairs. When he opened the door he was surprised to find his middle daughter, Christine, standing on the steps.

"Is it okay if I drop in?" she asked anxiously.

"Oh, yeah. Sure." He hugged her and bustled her back to the kitchen.

"I brought these from the Daily Grind." She held up a white bag.

"Scones," he said, trying to act happy. "I'm getting into scones."

"These are wonderful. They have cranberries and walnuts in them."

"Can't beat that. I'll make some coffee. Is everything all right?"

"Of course." She laughed. "Can't I just visit?"

"Sure," he said, scooping out the Community. But Christine was the last one to just drop in.

Her eyes were investigating the kitchen. "Everything's pretty clean," she observed, as if she expected him to exhibit some kind of piggish, single-man, crude qualities.

"I eat a lot of meals out," he explained. He got a plate for the scones. "You like honey?" She did.

"Did you know I got accepted at LSU?" Christine asked. He was dismayed. "No, I didn't even know you'd applied. You want to go there? What about Tulane? Isn't that your first choice?" It certainly was his.

"I haven't heard from them yet," she said anxiously. "And originally I was going to share an apartment with Debbie, but now she's getting married and moving in with Marcos. A lot of my friends are going to LSU."

He hit the switch on the coffeemaker, hard.

"I don't think I have the brains for Tulane anyway," she added.

"Of course you've got the brains. Any dummy can graduate from Tulane. Look at me. The hard part is getting in. Besides, they make you work lots harder at LSU." He hoped these were good arguments.

"I'm also on the waiting list at St. Olaf's."

"Saint who? Who the heck is he?"

"I don't know. It's a college in Minnesota. One of the boys I met on my trip to France is going there."

"Minnesota," he repeated, incredulous. "Please pass me a scone."

"I'd like to see more of the world," she said.

They had a nice talk. He gave her some advice. LSU didn't

sound so bad, upon reconsideration. Anywhere in the state beat Minnesota. Christine thought her sister Debbie should wear white at her wedding even if she was five months advanced. Tubby had not thought about that, but he agreed. Collette was secretly smoking cigarettes and sneaking into bars—which he had suspected but not actually known.

"She has good sense though, don't you think?"

"Sometimes" was all that Christine would concede.

It was just a visit after all. After Christine waved goodbye he watched her slip lightly down the sidewalk. He could see the young woman taking shape. This morning, he felt useful.

On the way downtown to meet the time-share lady, Tubby stopped at a sandwich shop on Magazine Street to grab some lunch. His plan was a nice trout po-boy, but the proprietor, a young guy from Paradis who could cook fish in a hurry, greeted him by saying, "Fresh oysters today. Just got 'em in. What'll it be?"

"That sounds good," Tubby said. "On French, dressed, to go."

"Got you covered," the cook said, and reached for a loaf of bread about the size of a softball bat. He whacked off a third of it. Tubby watched him take a handful of sliced Creole tomatoes and shredded lettuce. He was thinking that oysters were really sort of unappealing when you met one by itself. The moon rock shell might be as big as your hand, and stuck fast to all manner of barnacles and calcified sea life. Grab it firmly and it would likely slice the heck out of your fingers. It took a character with a strong wrist and a stout blade to open one, and then what you had was a moist pale creature void of form. Yet he could think of no superlatives adequate to describe the pleasures of consuming one.

"What to drink?"

"Red drink, please," Tubby said. "I changed my mind. I'm just going to eat it here."

No sense wasting a pile of crisp, hot, juicy, just fried oysters. He sat at a little square table and unwrapped the paper around his sandwich. He sprinkled on some Crystal, made sure he had pickles, and rolled with it. Man, that bread was fresh.

"Good oysters," he called to the cook, scattering a few bread crumbs.

"I said you'd like them," the man agreed, busy with a pan of frying catfish.

Soon, a relaxed and generally laid-back lawyer located his recently polished Chrysler LeBaron, which he had gotten when he traded in his Lincoln Town Car, and cruised on down Magazine.

He looked serenely at the black-garbed youths sitting on the front steps of the Necromantic Gift Shop and Museum, and the midday drunks propped up against the several taverns and Middle Eastern groceries along the route. He shrugged off the cold wind from nowhere that whipped the live-oak branches above the street. With no sense of aggravation he passed a stalled city bus, bright red and coated with an advertisement for Rex crab boil, and a guy who had parked his car in the middle of the street so he could use the pay phone outside of the K&B. Once downtown, he zipped past the main branch of First Alluvial Bank two blocks from his office, and did not even think about the dwindling balance in the checking account he kept there. Tubby didn't actually start to get his first twinge of tension until he turned into the multistory parking garage of the Place Palais, the building downtown where lately he spent too little time working.

The building was practically deserted since no one with any brains was anywhere close to the central business district on the day before Mardi Gras. Half the attorneys in New Orleans were off skiing in Colorado and the other half were recovering from the Bacchus Ball or getting ready to ride that evening with the Krewe of Orpheus.

He gunned it around and around the spiral ramp, tires squealing, remembering how it felt when he was growing up to cruise the old muscle cars on the Avoyelles Parish quarter-mile. When he got dizzy, he parked. Whistling, he locked up the Chrysler and went for a ride in the talking elevators.

When the grand machine announced that he had reached the forty-third floor, he marched into the carpeted hall and to the handsome walnut doors upon which, in gold letters, "Dubonnet & Associates" was etched.

With some difficulty he managed to figure out how the key worked in the lock. This was usually his secretary's job, but Cherrylynn was off for the day (and the next and the next) and no telling where she was.

He hit the overhead lights and checked his watch. It was half past one, so his client, if she showed up, was due soon. The door to his private office stood open and he tossed his briefcase on the old cypress desk that was the centerpiece. And, as Tubby usually did when he first got to work, he went to the window that covered one wall and surveyed his domain.

The view this afternoon was dramatic and frightening. He hadn't realized how it had clouded up, but some bad weather was definitely passing through. The eastern part of the city all the way to The Rigolets was bathed in a soft golden sunlight, almost like a beach at sunset. To the west, however, there was a wicked billowing black mass of clouds, an advancing stampede that blotted out both sky and earth. A seabird's view of startling weather patterns was one of the major perks of this office: this sky looked not only scenic but particularly menacing. He could imagine the shock waves it was literally sending to all those sailboat captains out on the lake trying to get back to the harbor, not to mention the fear in the hearts of all the Carnival krewe captains who were trying to get their parades lined up and rolling.

Well, better to rain on Lundi Gras than Mardi Gras, he thought.

He heard noises in his outer office and stuck his head out to see if maybe he had a paying client after all.

A short round lady with a distressed look was standing uncertainly in front of Cherrylynn's desk. She was not too much older than Tubby, he figured, but wore her hair in a bun, which added a few years. She clutched an enormous white purse and squinted at him so intently that he checked his hair.

"Mrs. Lostus?" he inquired.

"Yes?" she asked, as if surprised that someone knew her name in this place.

"I'm Tubby Dubonnet," he explained.

"Oh, yes." She extended her hand in his general direction. "You're the lawyer I've come to see."

"Good." He smiled. He could appreciate a conversation like this. "Won't you come back into my office?"

"If you're ready for me," she said politely.

Tubby stood aside to let her pass, and when she didn't he said, "This way, Mrs. Lostus."

Thus prompted, she plodded past him.

"Take this chair, please," Tubby said. He put his hands on the back of one of the stuffed armchairs so that there would be no misunderstanding.

"Thank you," she said.

He circled behind her and settled at his side of the desk. He rested his folded hands in front of his chest.

"I understand you're having a problem with a time-share." He nodded at her with encouragement.

"Well, yes," she said, staring out the window. "It certainly does look like it's going to rain."

"I know," Tubby said. "Something pretty big seems to be blowing from the west. I didn't hear anything about it on the weather report. You bought a time-share?"

"Yes. This very attractive young man stopped me on the street. By attractive, I mean he had very nice manners, though he was certainly good-looking too. I was just walking along thinking about where to have lunch."

"Right." Tubby rearranged his hands and waited.

"He said, 'Excuse me, ma'am, I have to give you a ticket.'"

Tubby raised his eyebrows.

"And I said, 'What for?' I was quite surprised."

"And he said?" Tubby primed the pump.

"He said, 'I have to give you a ticket for being happy,' of all things. I wondered what he meant. But he said my ticket was a lunch ticket. I could use it to have a gourmet lunch at the Pirate Mansion. It would be Creole shrimp gumbo, he said. And, if I would watch a short video, I would also get a free VCR."

"Such a deal," Tubby commented.

"It sounded very nice," she said. "They even had a shuttle bus right there to drive me to the mansion. I wouldn't have gotten in, but there was this very sweet girl with him, and they had on these cute T-shirts that said 'Pirate Mansion' on them. It looked all right, and you just have to go with your instincts sometimes."

She sat there and stared at the pictures of ducks behind Tubby's head, lost in thought.

"Ahem," he coughed presently.

"I was just thinking that they must be very clever," she said.

"Would you like a cup of coffee?" Tubby asked. There must be some around here someplace.

"No, thank you. I'm on a diet." She smiled.

"You rode in the shuttle bus," he tried again.

"Yes, and we rode past all the famous places in the French

Quarter, and the little girl told me all about the sights. Well, finally we got to the mansion and went inside. There was a couple there, the Murchisons, and they took me into one of the units with a nice balcony and explained how everything worked."

"Did you get lunch?" Tubby asked.

"Yes, I did."

"How was the gumbo?"

"I thought it was quite good. Not very spicy at all."

"How nice."

"And they showed me a film about the mansion, and I bought a week."

Tubby nodded. He understood how it had happened.

Suddenly there was a loud crack of thunder, and a waterfall of rain slammed into the window. Both client and lawyer jumped.

"My my," she said. The city was no longer visible. "You certainly have odd weather here."

"Very odd," he agreed.

"Well," she continued, returning her eyes to his, "we looked at my unit. It wasn't the prettiest of course because those cost too much, but it was clean. They explained all the rules. About how I could actually own the apartment, just like a condominium back home, but only for one week a year. And that week would be mine, always."

"You paid them?"

"I wrote a check for fifteen thousand dollars." Her brow furrowed.

"Have you had second thoughts?"

"Yes," she said regretfully. "I called my son as soon as I got back to my hotel room. You see, I had thought we could take vacations here together. But he got very upset. He looks after me. But it seems he does not want to vacation with me to New Orleans every year. I didn't know what to do so I took a walk. And I got to talk to Mr. Haywood, the bellboy at the hotel. It seems funny to call him a bellboy because he's a grown man. He told me that it is very hot here in New Orleans during the third week of August."

"That's the week you bought?" Tubby chuckled.

"Yes," she said defensively.

He composed his face. "It is indeed warm here at that time of the year. Do you want to get out of the contract?"

"Yes, I do," she said. "I promised my girlfriend, Sophie, that we would go to Las Vegas together next Christmas, and I realize now that I've just spent all my money."

"Okay, let's see how much of it we can get back."

"I hate to be this way. The Murchisons were so nice."

"They'll get over it, Mrs. Lostus. Did you happen to get their first names?"

Collette's friend Leila had a car, a really funky Mazda, and picked her up at around two o'clock. When they got to Norene's house they found a backyard full of kids. A couple of the boys were even swimming, and some others had stripped down to bathing suits and were showing off their winter tans. It was actually getting cloudy, however, and the main action was around the blue and white Igloo full of Bud Light.

Norene jumped up and hugged Collette and Leila when they came through the gate in the wooden fence.

"I was afraid you wouldn't come," she said. "We desperately need more girls. Come on and I'll introduce you to some of the guys. They go to Tulane."

"Ooooh," Collette said. Tulane. Big deal. She rolled her eyes.

So she met Bradley, who was not too tall but was really cute. He had brown hair and about two days' worth of whiskers on his chin.

"Hey," he said, smiling to exhibit his white teeth. "You wanna sit down?" He patted the empty part of the vinyl recliner he was resting on.

"I'd like a beer first," she said.

He asked her to bring him one, too.

After she fished two dripping bottles from the ice chest, she consented to rejoin him. At least he twisted off the cap for her.

"Where are you in school?" he asked while running his fingers through his hair.

"At Newman," she said. "I graduate in May." That was stretching the truth by about two years.

"Going to college?" he asked.

"Sure," she said. "Somewhere away from here."

"What's wrong with here?" he asked.

He turned out to be nice, though conceited, and he won points by telling his friends to quit splashing water on her.

It would have been really pleasant except that it started to rain, and they all had to go inside.

Norene tried to get everybody to play Pictionary, which was fun, but a couple of the boys were really drunk and started tearing up Norene's parents' den. They were throwing the couch pillows around, causing the lamps to rock back and forth, and they broke some kind of souvenir glass. It got too loud for Collette and she went looking for Leila to see if she was ready to go home. Unfortunately, Leila had already left without telling her, which was typical.

Collette plopped down angrily next to Bradley. He was telling jokes with one of his friends. He noticed her sour expression and offered his services. She said she was ready to leave, and he said sure, he would drive her.

One step out the front door, however, their plans changed.

It was pouring down rain, and the wind was whipping the trees around in a frightening way. There was water in the street, and they watched a car move through it slowly, pushing out a wake. Bradley's Nissan was parked in a low spot by the curb, and he ran screaming across the lawn to find that there was already water over his floorboards. After he got done cursing and hopping around, he got his frat brothers to help him push the crippled car into the driveway. When he inspected the saturated carpets he almost broke into tears.

In the meantime, the water rose another inch in the street,

and Bradley began to fret that the slight elevation of the driveway might not save his car much longer. He ran inside dripping and told Collette, who had been watching stoically from the window, that he would call a cab and try to get them both home. He knew a guy with some kind of a tow truck who he could get to come after his car, if they hurried.

He got busy signals at two cab companies before he finally got lucky.

8

Before the lights went out, things were going very smoothly in the vault. Blotting out the drone of the generator with earplugs, Big Top methodically applied the business end of the big Hilti drill to the locks of the safe-deposit boxes, grinding them to oblivion. He moved slowly along the wall, beginning at the top of each row and working downward to the floor, while Monk and LaRue ransacked each box and put everything they judged to be of value into a pair of canvas mail sacks. Mostly they were finding jewelry, cash, and rare coins.

"Here's a bottle of pills," Monk yelled, holding up an unlabeled brown plastic vial.

LaRue pointed to the bag, and in it went.

Most of what got left behind were papers, though LaRue scanned them all, and he kept a few.

They allowed James to go home at the end of his shift, after making Corelle clock in. To be sure that the SecureGuard headquarters was still cool about the cameras going on and off, they got Corelle to report in. LaRue sat next to him in the booth while he made the call, his handgun pointed at Corelle's crotch.

"These TVs is going nuts again," Corelle told the base.

"No wonder," the guy at headquarters said. "We've got a downpour here you wouldn't believe. Lights are going off all around town."

Corelle condensed that message when he hung up.

"He ain't worried. It's raining," he told LaRue.

The trio had completed most of one whole wall. Just three more to go. Corelle watched them sullenly from the floor where he had been told to sit and be quiet. The bags were bulging with goodies, and all three burglars were feeling the constant adrenaline rush of an excellent score when the lights went out.

Big Top looked up but kept on drilling with the power from the generator. LaRue tapped on Monk's shoulder and told him to keep filling the bags, while he pushed Corelle back to the dark booth.

Inside, all the TVs were dead, though a couple of green and red lights glowed on the alarm system's control panel.

"Call in," LaRue insisted to the guard.

Corelle picked up the phone and pressed the number.

"Line's dead," he said, and shrugged.

"Your new job is holding the flashlight," LaRue told him. "Looks like the weather is on our side." He allowed himself a thin-lipped smile. He was thinking they could spend the night cleaning out all of the boxes and maybe even take a crack at the vault just for the hell of it on the way out.

He was wrong, as they found out twenty-five minutes later. It came to Big Top's attention that there was water on the floor when he set the drill down for a second and got knocked for a somersault by some unseen powerful numbing force. He came back alive with Monk shaking him. LaRue was trying to get the damn generator turned off without electrocuting himself in the process.

Corelle, the security guard, was face down where he had fallen. He had made an abortive attempt to bolt the room in the confusion, and LaRue had clubbed him with the butt of his pistol. The water was now about an inch deep and rising fast to cover Corelle's ears.

"Mama," Big Top moaned, shaking his head, then his fingers.

"You stopped breathing there for a minute," Monk informed him.

"Whoa," Big Top crooned.

LaRue kicked a switch with his boot heel, and the roaring machine shuddered and died. They were left in a sudden silence, until the sound of trickling water got their attention.

"We've got what we came for," LaRue said. "Looks like the party's over."

"Can you walk?" Monk asked Big Top.

"I think so," Big Top said. He tentatively rose to his feet and leaned on the wall.

"Let's get all our stuff out of here," LaRue said.

"What about the guard?" Monk asked, indicating the limp wad on the floor.

"Leave him," LaRue said.

"He'll drown, if he ain't dead already," Monk observed.

LaRue splashed over to the fallen security man and pressed his wet boot squarely on the man's neck. He gave a quick jump that produced a brutal snapping sound on the floor.

"I guess we leave him," Monk said, wiping water from his eyes. "He'll be a hero now."

9

So far Bourbon Street had been a bummer. Marguerite had started out with high expectations on Sunday night. She showered off all the grubbiness from her taxi ride. After putting on a white cotton outfit she had bought for this trip, she ascended to the hotel's open-air rooftop bar. She climbed onto a tall stool, allowing the hem of her dress to rise and show off her two best features, ordered a tequila sunrise, and watched a handsome executive-type man swim. But he toweled off and left. So she allowed herself to get into a long conversation with a salesman from Michigan who finally moved to the stool next to hers. He ordered them both pink rum drinks in tall glasses. Together they soaked up the humid evening breeze, a wall of clouds moving in, ships moving slowly up the river, and the strings of lights flickering on the bridges.

He had an unusually strong chin, a roving Adam's apple, and slightly wild eyes, but he might do. The good-looking swimmer returned, dressed in beige slacks and a blue cotton blazer, and went to sit at the other end of the bar with a woman who had obviously been waiting a long time for him, so he was off the list. Marguerite accepted another of the syrupy rum drinks.

At a table near the pool, two men in business suits were talking seriously.

"It's the deal of a lifetime," she heard one say. "The oil's ready to come gushing out of the ground. If you can just make it all legal."

"I don't think that will present much of a problem," the other man, hair streaked with silver, replied.

By then it was completely dark, and Marguerite was thinking of dinner by candlelight. But the man with the wild eyes got weepy and started confessing about his wife back home. Off balance and frustrated, Marguerite stomped back to her room and ordered a pizza. The bellhop, Dan, had recommended that she call Mama Rosa's, and he was the one who brought it to her door.

She tipped the friendly fellow a dollar and got a courtly bow in return. With David Letterman for company, Marguerite ate as much as she possibly could. It was self-destructive, she knew, but she was feeling blue. She also raided the mini-bar in her room for wine coolers and vodka and cranberry juice.

She fell asleep with a glass in her hand.

The next morning, Marguerite woke up late, with a large headache, all alone, and the weather was crummy. At least it was so cloudy and gray that it might as well have been raining. She took a quick angry look outside and jerked the curtains shut. She ordered room service for breakfast, and it was not very good.

But the big pot of coffee they left with her restored her a little, and after she pushed the tray away she decided she might as well check out her very own second-floor balcony. As soon as she stepped outside and leaned over the rail, things started to get more interesting.

Attracted by her red silk bathrobe, some passersby below tried to engage her in conversation. Her spirits brightened when one man suggested she take it off. She twitched her hips experimentally, and he left laughing. After a while someone tossed a string of beads at her, and she put them on, working the plastic clasp under her hair. A little later she took them off and threw them across the street at a man looking at the pictures of strippers on the wall outside the cabaret. Bombed him right in the back of the head. This became a game.

There sure were plenty of weirdos walking around down there. Africans in tribal dress. Weight lifters in tutus. Kids tap-dancing on the sidewalk, until the hotel staff ran them off. Girls with earrings all over their faces.

But then it started to rain for real, and she had to run back inside to her dull room.

Two men scampered back to their lodgings from the Lundi Gras pageant at the river which had been interrupted by the sudden rain. They were leaping over puddles in the streets of Paris. That's how they felt, weaving and laughing down the cobblestoned alleyways of the French Quarter. Edward and Wendell had had a lunch of raw oysters for breakfast and after-dinner drinks for lunch. The stock market had become a foreign concept. The important issue was where to dine later—whether to eat *haute* at Arnaud's or *bas* at the Acme. But now was a good time to head home and be dry, back for a couple of hours of vigorous rest at the grotto, as they referred to their mysterious apartment at Lafitte's Lair.

The world that Willie LaRue found when he splashed his way to the brass and glass exit of the First Alluvial Bank was not the same one he had left four hours earlier. Monk and Big Top were pushing the generator and tool chest through the elevator lobby behind him, making gentle waves through the half-inch or so of brown water that was pooling in lazy swirls atop the marble floor and draining musically down the steps to the basement and into the deeper crevasses hidden by the elevator doors.

Everything that LaRue could see was wet. The street had become a canal, its shores marked by the rows of beached cars with water lapping their hubcaps. The sidewalk was submerged in most places. A UPS truck driver, frantic to escape the flood, blew a futile horn and slalomed through the intersection, sending a wave splashing over the doorsills of the storefronts facing the street.

LaRue unlocked the bank's solid doors with the key he had taken from Corelle. He wasn't worried about setting off any alarm. He doubted if anybody would respond, even if the damn things were working.

"What happened?" Big Top asked in awe, staring at the curtain of rain falling straight down from heaven. Grape-sized water bullets rebounded six inches when they hit, making the murky brown sea froth and boil.

"I don't know," LaRue said, finding himself disturbed at some deep primal level.

"Let's run for the van," Monk suggested. "This is just one of them crazy New Orleans downpours. It'll let up in half an hour."

"We sure as hell can't stay here," LaRue said, and set his jaw. He stepped out into the torrent, hugging the side of the building and dragging a heavy canvas sack full of loot.

It was difficult making any headway. The little wheels of the tool chest, with the second bag of booty riding on top, kept getting hung up on things hiding under the water. The three men, despite the limited protection of the tall buildings, were taking a pounding from the relentless rain. Their mission became manifestly senseless when they rounded the corner and saw that their van was gone. What they would never learn was that it had been towed for the difficult-to-foresee offense of parking on a parade route two hours before a parade. The robbers, however, had no idea whether their getaway vehicle had been stolen or had washed into Lake Pontchartrain, but it was gone.

LaRue looked helplessly at the sodden office workers who had waited too long to go home and were now huddled for shelter in doorways up and down the street. Some pointed and laughed at them, amused by the idiocy of moving machinery and packages in a deluge. Two young guys and a girl, pants rolled up above the knees, splashed happily down the middle of the street. All of the traffic lights were red. The robbers were calf-deep in water, and the heavens were wide open, joining earth, sky, and the nearby Gulf of Mexico into ecstatic congress.

A stubby pirogue piloted by a bare-chested man with a gray beard sailed past them, navigating the center of Carondelet Street. He waved at them amicably, paddling with graceful strokes.

"Let's get the hell out of here. Screw the generator and the tools," LaRue shouted. "Help me carry this bag."

Big Top helped and ended up with the whole sack on his shoulders. Monk got the other one off the tool chest. "I sure do hate to leave the tools here," he said.

"You can buy plenty more tools once you get back to the sticks," LaRue told him angrily. "Let's go."

Safari-like, the party sloshed off down the street.

"Here comes another boat." Big Top pointed behind them.

Two college boys in bathing suits were zipping down the street in a shiny aluminum canoe. They were doing acrobatics with their paddles and yodeling with their mouths open to drink in the rain. They had a case of Abita Beer between them, and they were looking for adventures and girls to save.

"Don't lose the damn bags," LaRue screamed, and left Big Top and Monk on the sidewalk. He struggled into the current and waved his arms like a windmill at the canoe. Obligingly, the boys steered at him and dug in their paddles to come alongside.

"Need help?" the one in front called.

LaRue didn't answer. He just gripped the boy's ears and hair and pulled him headfirst into the water.

"Steal the boat!" he yelled at his cohorts. While they splashed into the deep water to comply and to stow their treasure aboard, LaRue advanced on the boy in the canoe's stern. Alarmed by the loss of his mate, the young man raised his paddle in defense. LaRue grabbed it and yanked hard and tumbled the boy over the side.

The dethroned sailors struggled to regain their footing while Big Top and Monk clambered aboard. LaRue whacked at the bare-backed youths with the flat of the paddle until he had driven them to the sidewalk. Then he jumped in, gasping, and started stroking. Helplessly, the boys watched their vessel disappear toward Canal Street.

10

Hossein heard the call on his radio. He was parked in the K&B lot on Napoleon, trying to decide if he should just quit for the day and try to get home to Harahan, or whether he should roll down his window and acknowledge the fat lady with a plastic bag on her head who was thumping on the glass demanding that he give her a ride. He didn't want anyone that wet getting into his cab, especially because he thought she was probably only going a block or two anyway. Cab needed on Versailles Boulevard, his radio informed him, and he snatched the microphone.

"Three-two-oh. I can do the pickup on Versailles in five minutes."

"It's all yours, three-two-oh," the dispatcher replied.

It could be a trip to the airport. Rich people lived on Versailles Boulevard.

He gunned the engine, impervious to the woman angrily pounding on his hood, and splashed through a shallow lake in the parking lot. The rain was coming down in sheets and drumming on his roof. Hossein had to cut off a bus to make a U-turn, and his White Cloud Caddy did a wide slide on the slick asphalt and sent a monster wave over a dog and his master on the sidewalk. Praise Allah, this was a lot of rain.

It took more than the promised five minutes to get there because all of the cars on Claiborne Avenue were crawling along, intimidated by the rising tide that was obliterating the curbside lanes. Hoss tried switching his lights on and off and blowing his horn, but nobody would move out of his way.

At last he reached Versailles, which was entirely covered by water. He shot up it like a speedboat on the lake, wake arching behind him, looking for the address. Stopping in the center of the street, he blew his horn.

The door of the two-story brick home flew open and his two fares, towels covering their heads, ran toward him on the slate walkway. They had no luggage, meaning no airport trip, but anyone in this neighborhood ought to be a good tipper.

Collette and Bradley vaulted the last big puddle and fell into the back seat of the Cadillac. She was laughing. He was miserable.

"Wheee!" she screamed, flinging water everywhere.

"Where to, sir?" Hossein asked the young man.

"We're just trying to get home," Bradley said. "My car's flooded and I'm going after a tow truck. But I guess we'll take her home first." He glanced at Collette with some annoyance, which she failed to notice.

She gave the cabdriver her address.

"That's not very far," Hossein commented.

Bradley told him that he lived out by the lake.

"That's a little better," the driver said, only partly mollified.

"This sure is some rain," Bradley said.

"Yes, sir. I have not seen much worse. It may be a flood."

Indeed, a car up ahead had its emergency flashers on and was refusing to cross a particularly long pool.

"Sissies," Hossein spat. He turned off onto a side street. "I do not think this will make for a good Mardi Gras," he said. His taxi was fishtailing on the narrow street, almost colliding with the rows of cars parked along the sides. Collette grabbed the strap above the door for security.

"I bet you guys are really busy," Bradley called to the front seat. "I couldn't even get through on the phone to the other companies."

"Very busy, sir. Everybody wants to ride a taxi when it rains. You must be very careful whom you pick up though."

"What do you mean?"

"People want rides into the projects, where they rob you. You can't pick up everybody."

"How do you know we won't rob you?" Collette asked, holding tightly to the strap.

"Oh, miss, I know." Hossein laughed. "I can look at you."

"What he means," Bradley explained to the dummy, "is he doesn't pick up black people, isn't that right?"

"That's right, sir. Very seldom. One must be practical."

"I can't believe I heard that," Collette cried. "You don't pick up black people? I'm sure that's illegal."

"Well!" Hossein clamped his jaw shut and shook his head.

"C'mon, Collette," Bradley said. "Get real. Once you let

somebody in your cab you're at their mercy. He's right to be careful."

"Of course you should be careful," she said angrily, "but you can't judge whether someone is dangerous by the color of their skin."

"I bet you can ninety-nine percent of the time," Bradley said.

"I can't believe you're saying this," Collette shrieked. Didn't these people know what century this was? And Bradley was supposedly from Ohio.

"I must say he's quite right, ma'am," Hossein chimed in. "Colored people are not at all to be trusted."

Collette refused to look at either one of them. Seething, she stared out the steamy window at the rain pouring down. "You're both idiots," she whispered.

"No, we are the wise ones," Hossein said, gunning his engine to plow through a long lake that stretched the length of the block.

A huge wave washed over the windows, frightening Collette so much she almost jumped across the seat into Bradley's arms. She caught herself just in time.

"Whoa," Hossein cried when he realized that his front wheels were not responding to the steering wheel.

Like an old expiring beast, the engine coughed, bucked, sputtered, and died. The Cadillac floated on a few feet and stopped.

"Oh, no," Hossein moaned.

"Are we stuck?" Bradley asked.

Collette wiped the fog off the glass to try to figure out where they were.

"I think this is Calhoun Street," she announced.

It was a residential block crowded with shotgun houses built close to the sidewalk. People were hanging out on the porches of some of them watching it rain. Now they were watching the stranded White Cloud Cadillac.

Hossein tried the ignition but got no more than a red light on the dashboard.

"Oh, no, very bad," he crooned again.

"Wow, this looks like a really crummy neighborhood," Bradley reported. "What the hell are we gonna do?"

"Look!" Collette exclaimed, pointing to their feet where the blue carpet was being stained a deep indigo by water seeping in from below.

"There's like two feet of water out there," Bradley estimated.

Hossein looked forlornly at the brown faces watching them from the porches.

"Oh, no," he groaned miserably, and pounded his fists on the steering wheel. His banging was drowned out by the din the rain made beating down on the car's roof.

11

Ignorant of his daughter's plight, Tubby relaxed when his client walked out of his office at four o'clock. Touched by her story but glad to be rid of her, he waved and went back to his desk to stare at the downpour outside the window. He toyed with the $2,000 check she had given him as a retainer and thought it was going to be hell driving home.

Once he got there, however, a warm house and a big pot of chili he had made on Saturday afternoon from his special recipe awaited him. He might catch a basketball game on TV or track down his friend Raisin Partlow and see what he had on his mind for Fat Tuesday. He could take care of Mrs. Lostus's problem on Wednesday, if he could find a judge, that is.

"Mr. Dubonnet?"

He jumped and came close to injuring his nose where he had pressed it against the window glass.

"The elevators don't seem to be working," Mrs. Lostus announced in a soft voice.

Neither were the phones, it turned out.

This had happened before in the Place Palais building, and it had taken a long time to get fixed. On a holiday, the outlook was dismal.

"How about a drink?" Tubby suggested.

"Well, maybe a Coke," she said.

"I'm having something stronger," Tubby said. He opened the small oak cabinet beside his sofa that hid a bar and extracted a bottle of W. L. Weller with a couple of inches left in it.

"Not much of a party," he said, opening her can of Coke and pouring it over ice.

With a faint wheeze and a click, the air-conditioning shut down.

A wave washed against the window, and it visibly vibrated.

"At least we've got lights," he said.

They flickered.

"Who would think life could be so complicated," she added.

Tubby knocked back his drink and collected his briefcase.

"C'mon," he said. "There's nothing to do but start walking down the stairs. Maybe the elevators are working on another floor."

"Okay, but my feet aren't so good. I've got a fungus in my big toenail." She made that point again after they had opened the door marked "Emergency Exit," which let them into the bare concrete stairwell, and descended two flights.

"Just forty-one more to go." Tubby tried to cheer her up.

● ● ●

Nothing had ever seemed so monotonous. Nothing had ever taken so long. Mrs. Lostus held tight to the handrail and took one careful step at a time, leading off with her left foot and waiting for her right to catch up.

Tubby tuned out her complaints at floor 38, his own sore hamstring at 31, and decided to desert her at 25.

They had been joined for part of the journey by two young travelers, law school types, Tubby judged, forced to stay late in the office after all the partners had long since departed. They all swapped stories about where they had come from and theories about what they might find at the bottom. But the strangers were moving at a faster pace, and soon their voices could no longer be heard below.

Finally, at the thirteenth floor, Tubby and Mrs. Lostus encountered a security guard who confirmed that the building was not working due to extraordinary flooding in the streets. He guided them through normally locked doors to the parking garage and left them to continue their slow walk downward.

Tubby sprawled on the hood of his car on the third floor. He unlocked the door with fumbling fingers, and gratefully collapsed in the driver's seat. He leaned over to push open the passenger door for Mrs. Lostus when she closed the hundred-step gap between them. In time, she flopped beside him with a loud "Whoowee! I'm pooped!"

He cranked the engine and flipped on the air conditioner. He instantly felt better to be in charge of machines that worked again. Joyfully, he drove them to the ground floor, where they found out what all the trouble was about.

"This is big," Tubby said.

Mrs. Lostus bent over the dashboard and peered through the windshield. Inches from the LeBaron's front tires was a swirling soup of impure water floating plastic cups and Pepsi cans. It reminded her of something she had seen growing up in Goose Creek, Kentucky, and about which she had had nightmares most of her life.

She started screaming.

Unprepared, Tubby jumped so that his head hit the roof and he nearly screamed himself.

"For goodness sake," he pleaded. "It's just a rainstorm. It happens all the time here."

"Like that?" She pointed hysterically at the main channel, which to Tubby appeared to be about two feet deep in the middle of the street.

"Well, that sure is a lot of rain," he conceded. "Lemme go take a closer look."

He got out of the car and stood in the garage driveway at water's edge, trying not to get his shoes soaked.

A woman, blouse pasted to her body, was pressing through the stream with determination in the vicinity of where the sidewalk should be, water just below her knees.

"C'mon in," she invited Tubby. "You won't melt."

"What's the temperature like?" he asked.

"Not too bad. A little cool maybe." She splashed on.

"What should we do?" Mrs. Lostus called out the car window.

The rain was still pouring down. In Tubby's experience floods, once begun, did not end until at least a couple of hours after the rain stopped. It took that long for the mammoth pumps that guarded the city to suck the overflow out of the reclaimed swampland that constituted the Big Easy and push it uphill and over the levee to Lake Pontchartrain. Once it got there it would nurture blue crabs and nutria and all manner of other local delicacies before flowing back into the Gulf of Mexico.

The choices as he saw them were to stay put in the garage for, quite possibly, the rest of the night, with Mrs. Lostus, minus any food or drink—or wade four or five blocks to the French Quarter, where there were restaurants, bars, Mrs. Lostus's hotel, and more diverting companionship. This overflow must be localized in the downtown area, because everyone knew the French Quarter never flooded.

"Let's take the plunge," Tubby said.

He had to talk her into it, but she wanted to go to the bathroom and surely did not want to remain in the garage and miss all her shows.

While Tubby parked the car again a little higher up the ramp and locked his briefcase in the trunk, he tried to buoy his client's spirits with anecdotes about past floods and hurricanes. Her expression was troubled when he strung his shoes round his neck and rolled his pants legs above his white knees.

Mrs. Lostus said she was game for the trip, but she had no interest in taking off her Nikes, which she had recently purchased at the Payless Shoe Source near her home. They could just get wet. Same with her orange J.C. Penney slacks. She expected her lawyer to demand reimbursement for her dry cleaning bill from the time-share people.

"Ready, my dear?" Tubby asked gallantly.

Hand in hand, like a pair of bad schoolchildren, they stepped out of the sanctuary of the Place Palais garage and waded into the storm, guided through the drenching rain by the distant flashing neon of Canal Street.

"I don't like this," Mrs. Lostus said immediately. "Oh, this water is cold." Memories of Goose Creek were coming back.

Tubby tried to comfort her, but her complaints did not stop. He had not realized, standing back in the garage, that there was a current in this water, and it was running against them. Their progress was very slow, and before they had made the first block Mrs. Lostus gave a shriek and plopped down backwards into the grimy soup. She floundered about, unsuccessfully trying to keep her purse above the surface, while Tubby strained to help her get erect.

"I stepped off the curb, I think," she sobbed when she regained her feet.

Tubby got his arm around her waist and propelled her forward once more.

"Oh, oh," she moaned with each step. Whiskey and dry clothes seemed very far away. Two more miserable, sodden humans would be hard to imagine.

"It's a boat!" Mrs. Lostus screamed, pointing out a canoe bearing down upon them.

"It sure is," Tubby said. "Hey, guys!" he hailed the vessel.

There were three men in the canoe. They heard Tubby calling but kept paddling on a course down the middle of the street.

"Hey, guys! Help this woman!" Tubby yelled.

The men kept stroking, and even veered toward the far side of the channel. Clearly these fellows did not plan to rescue a pitiful damsel in distress.

"C'mon, men," Tubby pleaded. "Those bastards are going to pass us up," he said to Mrs. Lostus.

"Like hell they will," she exclaimed. Breaking free from Tubby, she plunged into the street, where the water quickly rose above her waist. Hands waving in the air, she leaned into the flow and struggled to intercept the passing boat.

"Hey, Mrs. Lostus," Tubby yelled. Swearing, he stepped off the curb to follow her.

He saw her make a grab for the aluminum gunwale and get her hand on it.

He heard one of the men say, "Let go, lady."

He saw the man in the back raise a gun and point it at Mrs. Lostus and pull the trigger.

He heard the report, quickly dampened by the rain, and he saw Mrs. Lostus sink beneath the surface. The canoe sailed on.

Tubby dove headfirst into the stream and thrashed about blindly, groping for his companion.

He felt a shoe and latched onto it, but the foot slid out. He came up for air, holding a wet brown Nike.

Desperately, he went under again, reaching here and there for Mrs. Lostus. Between dives he could barely make out the faraway canoe sailing across Canal Street; then it was gone. He could not find his client.

Tubby stood in the middle of the flood, clutching her shoe, yelling incoherently at the rain.

12

Oblivious to the state of his clothing and the dazed stares of other refugees flattened in doorways, Tubby splashed and swam to Canal Street. Here the many bayous converged to form a shallow brown sea. Stalled buses lined the neutral ground. The drivers were still in some of them, faithfully guarding the Regional Transit Authority's property, and a few passengers had remained aboard others. There was a pay phone outside Rubenstein's, and Tubby pressed 911. It rang and rang, but there was no answer.

He hung up and sagged against the pole. Absently, he patted his pockets and found that he still had his wallet, checkbook, and keys, and the trainman's pocket watch his father had given him. He couldn't make himself open the case to see how soaked it was. He still had his shoes, tied together and draped over his neck. All he had lost was his client, who had been murdered.

Assessing his situation while he caught his breath, he could think of nothing to do but keep going and bring the problem back to Dan the doorman, where it had all begun.

He took a first step, but a white flash, followed immediately by a crash of thunder, sent him jumping back for the telephone pole which stuck out of the water like the mast of a sunken schooner. More rain came down in sheets. It was hard to find air to breathe. This fact intrigued him, as an old student of New Orleans precipitation, but he was too agitated to dwell on it and cupped his hands over his mouth to create a pocket for oxygen. Urged on by new lightning crashes and the relentless wetness that enveloped him, he forced himself into the street and began making a ford toward the far shore, which had become completely invisible. This might be more than a normal rainstorm, he thought.

Though some of the store lights still shone brightly, there was evidence everywhere of a growing disruption. Dozens of cars were stranded in the street, empty as far as Tubby could tell, and some of them were slowly floating northward. He was not alone. There were other people wading purposefully through the tide, on emergency errands of their own. Passing a dead traffic light, he realized that he had reached the midpoint of the neutral ground. He clung to the cast-iron light pole, then fixed his sights on a flashing neon Dixie Beer sign in a drugstore, and waded on.

At last he was on Royal Street, in the old city, built on certifiably higher ground. It never flooded in the Quarter, they said, but today was different. Water covered the slate sidewalks, and shopkeepers were frantically erecting plywood barriers to try to keep the stuff out of their stores. In contrast to the practically deserted business district, the Quarter was packed. It was standing room only in the bars and groceries—anyplace that sold beer. Urchins, Mardi Gras revelers, and the rest of the city's cosmic debris cavorted mindlessly in the street.

The sounds of Bix Beiderbecke played from a hand-cranked Victrola on a balcony. Tubby knew he was losing his grip, but he focused on a single objective. His glare was fixed on the hazy outline of the Royal Montpelier Hotel. He was going to get the highest room his plastic could buy and deal with this situation from way up there.

The towering entrance was guarded by tall men whose turbans were covered by plastic bags. In case he was needed, a uniformed security guard was leaning against one of the marble pillars, sheltered by the portico, smoking a cigarette.

"You got a room, sir?" A liveryman blocked Tubby, who resembled a half-dead escapee from Angola.

"No, but I'm about to," Tubby replied, straightening up. He tried to brush past.

"Sorry, sir," the man said, his hand gently upon Tubby's heaving chest. "We're all full."

"I'm sure I can arrange something," Tubby said desperately.

"We're all booked, sir," the man repeated. "Sorry." He was not going to yield.

"Listen, you know Dan Haywood?" Tubby pleaded.

"Who?"

"Dan Haywood. He works here."

"The bellman?"

"Right. Big tall guy with a mustache?"

The gatekeeper nodded.

"Look, could you get him for me? Hey . . ." Tubby pulled

a spinachlike bill from his smelly wallet. He offered it to the man. "Tell him his lawyer is out here and needs help bad."

The warden of the gate looked disdainfully at the green wad in Tubby's hand and sniffed.

He flicked his head in rebuke.

"Wait here," he said, and withdrew into the dark dryness of the hotel lobby.

"Hell of a storm," the uniformed guard said to Tubby, making conversation.

"I can't remember anything like it," Tubby said. He wished he could stand under the awning beside the guard.

"May '95 was bad," the man said, scratching behind his ears, "but not this bad."

"No, I can't say I remember ever seeing the Quarter flood like this," Tubby said, edging closer.

"I heard they may cancel Mardi Gras," the guard said.

Tubby had forgotten all about Mardi Gras.

"They'll have to, if this keeps up," he said, stating the obvious. "Hey, mind if I come up on the steps out of the rain?"

"Oh, sure," the guard said. "At least until Mustapha gets back. Try not to drip on the rug."

"Right," Tubby said, hopping up. The hotel's red carpet was already quite damp. "I feel drier already." He shivered.

"Tubby, my man!" Dan's voice bellowed behind him.

The lawyer turned and beheld his savior.

"Come inside and dry off."

Tubby followed Dan as he would have Moses, wanting to weep and hug him.

The lobby was jammed. Every available seat, including

the surfaces of the coffee tables and the brass stand-up ash-trays, had someone squatting on it. People sat cross-legged on the floor, and rested forlornly on their luggage, where they had been stranded at checkout time.

Dan quickly gauged Tubby's condition.

"Follow me, sir," he said, taking Tubby's arm firmly. He led the lawyer behind the concierge's desk to the luggage storage room. In a cavern of dim shelves piled high with suitcases and tennis rackets, Dan pointed his limp friend to a tiny table shoved against the back wall. He pushed Tubby into a rickety wooden folding chair, swept away a tin ashtray full of cigarette butts, and pulled a fifth of Old Crow with two cloudy glasses from a lady's overnight case.

"Take a snort, boss, and tell me all about it," he said soothingly.

13

"For chrissakes, why'd you do that?" Monk exploded at
LaRue, staring back through the torrent where the woman
had disappeared into the murky water and where a large man
was waving his fist helplessly at them. In the middle of the
canoe Big Top, wide-eyed, was too awed by Rue's careless
violence to speak.

Rue wiped the pistol under his arm to get some of the water off and stuck it back in his pants.

"Shut the fuck up," he told Monk, "and watch where
you're going."

Their craft was drifting toward the picture window of a
fancy hatter's. Miserable, wet, and convinced that he might at
any moment be shot by a madman, Monk got back to work
with his paddle and straightened them up.

The canoe shot across Canal Street, scraping briefly over
a raised piece of roadway or something equally rough, and
zipped onto Bourbon, out of sight of the man with the raised
fist.

LaRue, in truth, was not feeling very well himself. Losing

the van was bad. He had also been afraid of water since he was a boy, and he was a poor swimmer. Shooting the woman had been dumb. He had been afraid she would capsize the boat. But he had to admit that blowing her head off was dumb. He hated himself when he made mistakes. Blame it on this unreal rain. The urge to retreat into painless sleep was very powerful.

He had no idea where they were going or where they could find a hole to hide in. At least it would be a while before the cops started to tail them. That was a plus. He was drowsy.

This place was full of crazies.

Two skinny blond kids, naked and apparently drunk, were having a water fight in front of a cigar store. A stocky man with black bushy eyebrows charged out of the shop swinging a broom handle at them.

"Quit making waves, damn it. You're washing water into my store."

They laughed and splashed into midstream, blocking the path of the canoe.

"Get out of the way," Monk yelled, gesturing with one hand while gripping the paddle in the other. He was terrified that Rue might start shooting again, wasting everyone they encountered.

"Come on in," one of the boys invited.

"Red Cross. Get out of the way," Monk cried.

Oblivious to any danger, they dove away just in time, and the canoe floated on, passing a world of windows full of faces, under balconies full of tourists in colorful rain gear with umbrellas held aloft.

"We ought to dock this baby somewhere," Monk said. "This current is probably pulling us into a huge drain."

Two policemen on horseback were dead ahead, moving slowly up the street. Monk shook Big Top's knee behind him and he in turn pointed the cops out to Rue.

LaRue seemed to be in a daze. Exasperated, Monk gestured his thumb left, and the canoe made an awkward sliding turn into St. Louis Street.

"We'll just zigzag around until we find someplace dry," he said.

"Right," LaRue mumbled. "We'll just zigzag."

Cheerful and quite tipsy, Edward and Wendell were sitting on the steps of their grotto, saying hello to the people who waded past in the flood. They were using an old-fashioned manual eggbeater to try to make a frozen daiquiri out of a lot of rum and the rapidly melting sack of ice they had bought at the A&P.

The water lapped peacefully just beneath their toes, carrying with it plastic bottles and cups. The rain came and went in sudden flurries, and every few minutes the wind kicked up and sent ripples and whirlpools down the street. A pretty girl wearing a tie-dyed top and green pantaloons rolled up high on her thighs walked past carrying a bedraggled beagle under her arm. She waved as she sloshed along, against a background of ancient pink brick.

"This is the wettest place in the world," Wendell observed.

"It certainly is," Edward agreed, tasting the concoction in the white saucepan between his knees. "Or maybe we've reached the end of the world."

"And only one pair of every species will be saved."

"Quite possibly that's us. What species do you think we are?"

"I don't know exactly," Wendell said, putting his finger beside his nose, "but look, here comes our ark."

Indeed, a canoe, rocking dangerously from side to side, was paddling their way.

"It appears to be full already," Wendell said sadly. "We'll just have to stay behind and drown in our little cave."

"Try this," Edward said, offering his companion a frosty glass full of purple liquid.

"Lovely," Wendell said, holding it up to the rainy sky. "Ahh, drown me," he cooed as he sipped it.

"Here, here, you're going to crash!" Edward waved at the canoe, which was bearing directly upon them.

Unheeding, the men on board brought it up hard against the steps with a loud grating of tin on granite. The man in front tried to get a grip on the second stone, failed, and locked his fingers around Wendell's ankle.

"Good sir, unhand me," Wendell protested, trying to stand up and reclaim his leg.

Already, however, the redheaded man in the middle had gotten one foot out of the canoe and onto the steps. Steadying himself with one hand on the boat rail, he got the rest of his body out, crowding Edward and his pot of daiquiris back into the apartment.

"Hey now. What's going on?" Edward demanded feebly while the robbers disembarked awkwardly but rapidly from their metal craft.

"Move along, sonny," LaRue ordered, focus restored. He made his voice like sharp steel again. Shedding water, he pushed Wendell hard through the door. "Who else is in the house?" he wanted to know. Outside, Big Top tied the boat to one of the front-door latches.

"What do you mean?" Edward asked excitedly.

"Nobody," Wendell said.

Big Top hoisted a wet canvas sack out of the boat and dumped it through the apartment doorway. He leaned back to get the other one.

"Both of you sit over there on that couch," LaRue ordered. "Monk, watch 'em."

Dripping as he went, LaRue made a quick search of the bedroom and small kitchen. Satisfied that the place was empty, he came back to confront the two surprised vacationers.

"We're moving in with you for a while," he told them. "Just do what we tell you to do and you won't get hurt. Okay?"

"Okay," Edward and Wendell said in unison.

"Fine," LaRue said. "Then let's all get settled in."

He sat down on a small Chippendale chair in the corner and lifted the telephone to see if it worked. There was no dial tone.

"Why don't you see what they got to eat in the kitchen," he suggested to Big Top.

"This is nice," Monk said. "You guys live here?"

"We're just in for Mardi Gras," Wendell said.

"The lights don't work?"

"No, they went out a little while ago."

"It's getting dark," Monk noted.

"There are some candles on the table over there." Edward pointed.

"That's great."

"Are you planning to be here long?" Wendell inquired politely.

Monk glanced at LaRue. "Depends on how long the flood lasts," he said.

"Where are you from?"

"Colorado," Monk lied. "You?"

"Atlanta," Wendell said.

"I like Atlanta."

"It's okay. Why'd you pick this place to barge in on?"

"Your door was wide open." Monk smiled.

"What are you guys? Bank robbers?" Edward inquired.

"What gives you that idea?" LaRue asked in that quiet voice of his. He leaned back and rested his boots on a wicker footstool. It served to put a temporary end to the conversation.

"We got some wine and vodka," Big Top reported, bringing out some bottles. "There's some leftover spaghetti and some crackers."

"Oh, there's lots more than that," Wendell said. "There are vegetables and some shrimp from the grocery store. And there's some meat in the freezer. I don't know how good it is.

It was here when we got here. It will all go to waste if it isn't cooked."

"Are you a cook?" LaRue asked.

Edward shrugged. "We had planned to cook some of the recipes in those old cookbooks in the kitchen. We just got back from shopping."

"Well, here's a drink anyway." Big Top passed around glasses. He included the two subdued tourists on the couch. "If we can't go anywhere, we might as well get drunk."

14

It was getting dark, and someone was beating on the window of the taxi. Hossein rubbed away enough condensation to see who it was. He refused to roll his window down.

"Oh boy," Collette said in disgust. She cracked hers an inch. A large black man, hunched over against the gale, stuck his eyes up to the gap in the glass.

"You need help?" he yelled.

"We're stuck," she said.

"I can see you ain't going nowhere. You want to come inside?"

Collette looked at Bradley, who looked back, noncommittal. Hoss would not acknowledge the invitation.

"You mean inside your house?" Collette asked.

"Yeah. Inside my house. The water is rising. Y'all are going to get mighty wet out here."

"Well, sure," Collette said.

"Okay. I can carry you. I can only fetch one at a time though."

"No, don't go," Bradley said urgently, gripping Collette's elbow.

She shot him her stern look.

"Ready when you are," she told the face in the window.

"Don't try to open the door," he said. "Just roll down the window and climb out."

She did as she was told and found herself sitting on a stranger's broad shoulders. Water over his belt, he slowly forded the street. With cautious footwork he first found the sidewalk and then the steps to his house. He stood on the bottom one, water to his knees, and set her down with a bump on the wooden porch. It was high and dry, out of the rain.

"Thank you so much," she said, extremely relieved to be standing on something solid.

"Go on inside and dry off," he called out on his way back to get the others.

She opened the torn screen door and stepped tentatively inside.

A big woman rose from the couch.

"Come on in, honey," she told Collette. "Junior, give her that chair and go find us a towel. The pink one."

Bradley arrived on the porch the same way Collette had, his dignity somewhat impaired.

"Thanks, man," he said. "I guess I could have made it myself."

"I was already wet," the big man said, climbing the steps. He showed Bradley through the screen door.

"Get him a towel, Junior." And the tall teenager with the shaved head sauntered again to the rear of the house.

"My name is Collette. This is Bradley, and we really appreciate your letting us in."

"I'm Noah Brownlee," the man said. "My wife is Paella. Your cabdriver won't come in."

"Why not?" Collette asked.

Brownlee shrugged. "Said he don't want to leave his cab."

Collette was wringing out her hair. "That's ridiculous. He might drown."

"Lot of foreigners ain't too bright," Brownlee said. He sat down with a thud on the couch and began unlacing his heavy shoes. Puddles formed around his feet.

"Lord, will it ever stop raining?" Paella asked, bustling in from the dark recesses of the house with a tray. She had glasses of hot tea for each of them.

"That man going to stay out there?" she asked.

"So he says," Noah told her. "Where did Junior go?"

"He's watching TV in the bedroom." Paella passed around the steaming glasses. "I think he's a little shy about having all this company."

With a grunt, Mr. Brownlee finally got his feet out of his wet shoes. He fell back against the plastic-covered couch cushion, satisfied with his accomplishment.

"I seen y'all hit that water. I knew you was going way too fast."

Bradley and Collette nodded in agreement.

"He shouldn't have come down this street anyway. Seems like it floods here every time it rains. Where do you live?"

The refugees told him.

"I don't see how they're going to get home tonight," Paella said.

Noah shook his head. "They can't. Might as well have supper with us."

"We couldn't," Collette said.

"It won't be any trouble," Paella assured her. "I make a big pot of red beans and rice with smoked sausage every Monday. And they're just about ready."

"I've really got to get home," Bradley said.

" 'Less you can fly, I don't see how you're gonna make it," Noah said. "Paella, you seen my cigarettes? I hate to think I run out, 'cause if I did I'll have to swim to the store." He looked at Collette and laughed. "Wouldn't that be funny? Do you smoke?"

"No," she said.

"People in my generation had lots of bad habits," he said. "I'm glad to hear you ain't got 'em."

"Can I use your phone, Mr. Brownlee?" Collette asked. "I've got to call my mom."

15

Tubby was starting to feel better. He had described the murder of Mrs. Lostus to Dan, and they shed a few tears for her. They said what they would do to the murderers if they ever caught them, and they shared a couple of drinks. They agreed that crime had gotten totally out of control.

"If it weren't for the good weather, I mean usually good weather, nobody would live here," Tubby announced angrily.

"'Where blackness is a virtue,'" Dan said solemnly into his glass. "Now what song is that from?"

In time, Wild Dan left Tubby with the bourbon bottle while he attended to his business in the lobby, and the lawyer drank off his chill. Then he scrounged up a dry pair of toreador pants, a ruffled silk shirt, and some shiny black lace-up boots left behind by a calypso band that had once played in the bar.

Tubby checked himself in a cracked mirror leaning against the wall and tried out what he remembered of his bossa nova repertoire.

"Zorro, my padrone." Dan clapped.

"Did you find me a room?" Tubby asked, hand on hip, elbow and knee counterpoised.

"Not yet," Dan said, helping himself to a tumbler of spirits. "The place is overflowing with guests. There are people in the lobby offering unlimited sums of money, their bodies, you name it, for a room key. Them who's got a chair are afraid to leave it to go to the can."

"Is it still raining?" Tubby asked.

"Buckets, son," Dan said, knocking back his whiskey neat. He wrinkled his mustache and sneezed. "Damn manager needs to turn up the heat in this place. Saves it all for the paying guests. No consideration at all for the workers."

"I suppose I could stick it out here," Tubby said, surveying the shelves packed with luggage. He could make a mattress out of a wide selection of carry-on bags.

"No, don't give it up yet. I've got my friends here." Dan gave Tubby a mysterious wink. "I ain't talked to all of 'em yet. We'll get you a bed, never fear."

"And something to eat," Tubby added.

"The kitchen ain't up and running yet, but I heard ol' Chef Fouise banging around in there cussin' up a storm, so I reckon we'll get it going soon."

A bell on the wall rang, and Dan hopped.

"Be cool, brother," he said in parting. "Ol' Dan will take care of everything. I own this place, man." He hustled back to the lobby.

Tubby flipped through the magazines stacked on an old steamer trunk. *Penthouse, Racing Form, Mother Jones.* He saw on each cover the back of Mrs. Lostus's head split by a dark red hole, sinking into the swirling water.

He found an orange furniture pad and wrapped it around himself for warmth. Seated again on his folding chair, shiny boots propped on the steamer trunk, he dozed off.

Dan's rough hand on his shoulder brought him back to life.

"Wake up, Tee," he said. "I got you a crib."

Tubby stretched.

Dan stood back, fist to his chin, and appraised him.

"My God, don't you look like a dandy. The cape is perfect. She's going to love you."

"Who is 'she'?" Tubby asked, yawning.

"Your roommate," Dan said, stuffing Tubby's wet clothes into a pillowcase. "I don't think these will ever come clean. I can run them through the hotel laundry and see what they can do. Unless you want to take them with you."

"Go ahead. I have a roommate?"

"Everybody is doubling up. And you are going to like this one. She's real nice-looking. She's all by herself, and she's been drinking all day."

"And she'll let me stay with her?" Tubby was dubious.

"She wants to see you before she commits, of course, but she trusts me. We've developed a very friendly relationship over the past two days. I told her what an important lawyer you are. That you're a gentleman. That you're desperate. I suggested you might pick up the tab for the hotel."

"The room has two beds?"

"You betcha, son. It's one of the best. It's a Mardi Gras special, with a balcony and everything. She reserved it months ago."

"Well, let's go and see if she'll have me." Tubby rubbed the sleep from his eyes.

"Only thing, I think you better lose the orange cape. It clashes with your pretty red trousers."

Tubby followed Dan through the lobby, weaving through clusters of people laughing over drinks and others curled up on the Persian rugs sleeping, all washed up by the storm. A few of the squatters, in honor of the season, were in costumes more outrageous than Tubby's own.

"The stairs are quicker," Dan said, and led them up the creamy marble steps.

Down a purple-carpeted hallway they went, until Dan stopped and rapped on the door of room 209.

"Who's there?" a woman asked.

"Room service. Your guest is here," Dan called.

The door flew open, and Tubby beheld a tall blue-eyed female dressed in baggy jeans and a bulky gray sweatshirt that hid her shape.

"What have we got here?" she asked loudly, checking out the large man in the undersized red pants.

Tubby blushed.

"This is Tubby Dubonnet," Dan interceded. "He's a lawyer with excellent manners. I vouch for him completely." Dan poked Tubby in the back and winked at Marguerite. "He got caught in the storm and is seeking shelter."

"Come in," she said, standing aside to let them pass. "I guess he's acceptable," she said to Dan. "Bathroom's to the left. Bar's straight ahead."

Dan pushed Tubby over the threshold.

"I really do appreciate this, Miss Patino," Dan said. "I know you haven't had much fun in New Orleans so far. If it ever quits raining, I know Tubby here will show you a real good time."

"Uh . . ." Tubby began.

"Now I gotta get back to work." Dan stepped into the hall. "Check you later," he said, cocking his finger at Tubby, and closed the door on them.

"Ahem," Tubby said, looking around.

"Don't just stand there," Marguerite said. "Fix a drink, pull up a chair, and tell me about yourself. Just make it entertaining."

She jumped onto one of the beds, strained to reach a plastic glass full of a golden liquid on the nightstand, and sat cross-legged on the spread, waiting.

"I have to call the police," Tubby said.

Marguerite put one hand over her eyes and with the other lifted the glass to her lips and drained it.

16

"Right," Tubby said to the police operator, trying hard not to shout his frustration. "Carondelet near Common Street. That's were she was shot. That's where the body disappeared in the water.

"Look, can you try to get this information to Detective Fox Lane in Homicide? Give her my name and this number?"

Slowly he read the hotel's number off the phone.

"Room two-oh-nine. . . . Right. . . . Thanks."

Marguerite was lying on her side, propped up on her elbow, listening and watching Tubby carefully.

"That's what happened to me today," he said.

She tossed the hair out of her eyes.

"I asked for action," she said, and held out her glass. "Pour me some wine, big guy."

Tubby opened the wooden cabinet that concealed a large TV, a bar, and a refrigerator. Her half-empty bottle of Chardonnay was floating in a stainless-steel ice bucket. He

fixed himself a glass by emptying two mini-bottles of Wild
Turkey.

Outside it was raining.

"It was nice of you to let me in." He served her.

"Do you always dress like that?" she asked.

"No." He laughed. "I stole them off the conga player in
the dining room."

"Speaking of which, did you see any food down there?"

"No, but I could sure use some."

"You got any dough?"

"Absolutely." He smiled, showing her the gold card in the
pocket of his ruffled shirt.

"Oh, goody," she said. "Let's make it a party."

Wendell carefully tapped the filé out of the cylindrical jar into
a teaspoon. It was a spice he was not familiar with, but the
recipe he had found for okra shrimp gumbo called for it, and
the man at the A&P where they had shopped earlier that
day—a long time ago, it seemed now—had known just what
they were talking about. Wendell was so absorbed in his culi-
nary endeavor that he had almost forgotten that he and Edward were prisoners and that their captors were getting
staggeringly drunk in the living room.

Or two of them were. Monk and Big Top had pushed the
furniture against the walls and between shots of vodka and
Scotch were leg-wrestling on the throw rug. Periodically they
would throw open the shuttered front door and thrash

around outside in the floodwaters, which remained on a level with the first doorstep. The rain was intermittent now, sometimes rolling down the street like a water cannon, sometimes stopping entirely.

As the evening wore on, more neighbors—a strange assortment of long-haired teenage kids with artfully torn clothing, lost-looking drunks, potbellied men in undershirts, and knights in black leather—were poking their heads outside and, in many instances, wading about. It being a fairly transient neighborhood, no one paid any special attention to the water antics of Monk and Big Top. Mainly they passed greetings and comments on the weather. The canoe moored to the front door was a conversation piece, but nobody tried to steal it or contest their ownership.

Edward had escaped to the bathroom to read a magazine in seclusion and get out of the range of the two crazy bank robbers. He was under orders to stay inside and away from the front door, and he had no immediate intention of challenging the rule. For one thing, he could not abandon Wendell. For another, jumping into the dirty water covering the sidewalk had no appeal to him whatsoever. For a third, he feared the bad guys, especially the one called Rue, who, thankfully, was off to himself in the bedroom.

LaRue had needed a nap, but he didn't want anybody to know. He collapsed on the four-poster bed and went numb. After about twenty minutes, the bright light in his brain switched on again, and he sat upright. Seeing that he was alone and secure, he straightened his clothes and began taking an inventory of the stolen loot. Dragging one of the wet sacks to the side of the bed, he inspected the booty piece by piece. He could see already that they were rich.

He had Krugerrands, diamond bracelets, emerald rings, fine silver, packets of currency, ruby brooches, gold pins, antique chessmen, solid bullion, pieces of eight, gem-encrusted cuff links, long strands of pearls, engraved pocket watches, and some legal documents rolled up in a scroll and tied with a purple ribbon.

The phone had come back on, and he tried to make his call twice. First he got no answer, which could mean there were still problems with the line. The second time, a woman whom he did not know answered, and he hung up.

It disturbed LaRue to be out of touch with the man who had conceived this operation, only because he wanted to bring it to a rapid conclusion. This involved turning over certain things and also getting paid in untraceable cash. He was not concerned about his present safety, however, and he did not mind making up the rules as he went along. Ever since he had backed a pickup truck over his father, LaRue had been able to make the tough choices. Upon reconsideration he had even decided that getting rid of the guard and the woman were smart things to do—calculated risks, so to speak. Sometimes people got in the way. He figured the chances of getting caught for either act were zero.

Edward's reverie in the bathroom was interrupted by a pounding on the door.

"The two debauchers," he said to himself.

He drew back the bolt and found Big Top, scrawny in his underwear, muddy and dripping copiously.

"What the hell are you doing in here, sleeping?" Big Top screeched.

"Just reading a magazine," Edward said truthfully.

"Tell you what," Big Top announced, pushing past him. "I'm going to take a shower and clean up for supper."

He stripped off his shorts and socks, hopping one-legged around the bathroom and banging into the sink. He threw his soggy clothes in Edward's general direction. "See if there ain't a washing machine around here, would you?"

"There's not," Edward said, offended.

"Then I'll wear some of your dry clothes. While I'm in here you can haul out your duds and I'll see what you got."

Big Top closed the door on him. Monk was stretched out in a wet spot on the floor, watching the ceiling fan rotate slowly in the breeze from the windows.

"Howya doin', buddy?" he inquired lazily as Edward stepped over him.

Edward did not reply. In the kitchen, Wendell was humming an upbeat tune and chopping onions and tomatoes.

"It'll be done soon," he said, intent on his work.

"It looks wonderful," Edward said. "But what about getting away?" he whispered. "Don't you think we should make a run for it?"

"But my soufflé is in the oven," Wendell said crossly.

"What are you making?" Edward asked.

"Cheese soufflé and Chicken Louisiane."

"Which is?"

"Oh, you fry up the chicken and then you put on the olives, and the artichokes, and the mushrooms, and a little sherry, and the secret ingredients, and that's what it is," Wendell said, dusting the flour off his hands. "You serve it on rice."

"It smells great. But you know they might kill us or something. I think we could slip out the front door."

"And go where? It's an ocean out there. Would you like some wine?" He poured a glass for himself from the bottle of Cabernet Sauvignon airing out on the Mexican-tiled counter.

"We could find a police station. There must be one around here. Or we could knock on doors until somebody took us in."

"And leave all of our stuff?" Wendell raked the tomatoes and onions into the iron pot simmering on the gas stove. He flourished his carving knife in the air.

"I don't think you're taking this very seriously," Edward complained.

Wendell took his friend by the hand. "We're in a flood, in New Orleans at Mardi Gras, and have been kidnapped by desperadoes. I should take that seriously? They don't seem so dangerous to me. Well, maybe that Rue, but not the other guys." He consulted his cookbook. "'Cook soufflé twenty to twenty-five minutes in a moderate oven,'" he muttered. "'Shrimp, ham, or chicken may be added.'"

"Look, Wendell," Edward began, but he was interrupted by Big Top bellowing from the bathroom, demanding clean clothes.

"Now he wants my clothes," Edward hissed.

Wendell shook his head distractedly. "I wonder if I burned that roux," he said.

Frustrated by his inability to formulate an escape plan, Edward went back to the living room, where Monk was now snoring on the rug, legs splayed out across the floor and a glass of ice cubes balanced on his rhythmically rising and falling stomach.

He went to the bedroom to retrieve his suitcase, planning to try to pawn off a pair of sweatpants and an old brown Chattahoochee River Race T-shirt on Big Top.

"Whaddya mean, you can't get us out of here," he heard Rue saying into the phone.

"We don't want to wait here too long." LaRue looked up at Edward. "This place is too populated." Addressing Edward, he said, "Get out of here until I'm finished."

Edward left, after getting an eyeful of all the gold and jewels and silver spread out on the bed.

"How long are they saying the flood is going to last?" LaRue continued. "You wanna meet me tomorrow at the spot where we planned? . . . No, I can't stick around here any longer. There were casualties. . . . You'll read about it in the papers. . . . You gonna be at this number? I don't want to deal with anybody else. . . . Right."

LaRue lit one of his hostage's Kamels and stood up. He tied the scroll up in the ribbon again and tossed it on the bed with the rest of the goods. He took a puff and decided to bring Monk and Big Top in to see what they had gotten. Let them each pick a piece, a stone or a bracelet. He didn't see how they would live to show it off, and a little sparkle might inspire them to run the last leg of this race.

On Annunciation Street there is a warehouse where they make Mardi Gras floats all year round. It is never so busy, of course, as during the countdown to Carnival, and with water pouring in from the street it crawled with activity like a stirred-up anthill. The screams of power saws and the banging of hammers almost made it impossible for Chesterfield to have a two-way conversation on his portable phone.

"We're taking them apart right now," he yelled. "That's right. We're taking off everything within three feet of the ground. It's flooding like hell here.

"Sure we can get them back together," he told the captain of the Krewe of Moravian Elves. "If you can make it stop raining, I can get you ready to roll in no time."

On the shores of Lake Pontchartrain, at a bar called Champs, a woman named Monique and her bartender, Jimmy, were nailing sheets of plywood over the windows. It was raining torrentially, and the wind was blowing armies of dark green waves into the shore. They crashed rhythmically into the bar's wooden dock and threatened to wash the slim woman and the pencil-thin bartender over the side.

"We'll never get them all covered, boss," Jimmy shouted,

spitting out a mouthful of warm brackish water. His fingers were bleeding from where wind-borne plywood had ripped them. He had mashed a thumbnail with the hammer, and he had twisted his knee on the slippery planks.

"We will too, by God," Monique replied between the tenpenny nails clenched in her teeth. Her dress was torn. There was a cut above her right eye where she had fallen and struck the railing. "This goddamn lake is not getting into my goddamn bar."

In the Irish Channel, at Mike's Bar, the card game continued. Larry had drifted ghostlike from behind the mahogany bar to stuff some rags under the doorsill. The howling wind outside was drowned out by Bobby Darin singing "Mack the Knife" on the jukebox. Judge Duzet was dealing down the river, and Mrs. Pearl was way ahead.

"Could we have something else to drink here, Larry, if it ain't too much trouble?" Newt asked.

"You need to put in your fifty cents," the judge reminded him.

"That's right, Judge. You watch him carefully," Mrs. Pearl said, lighting her Pall Mall. "Now deal me one of them aces you're holding under the deck."

Rounding Algiers Point in the black of night, the towboat *Prissy Ann* caught the wind broadside. Whitecaps slapped against the hull and broke over the deck, but it was the water and not the boat that gave way. A storm on the Mississippi River was nothing new to Captain Ambrose. His engines did not even hiccup, and his sturdy boat droned steadily on through the agitated dark sea.

A German shepherd paddling furiously across Earhart Boulevard in the dark encountered something unexpectedly human. It was floating, and he pressed his nose through the wispy hair and against the cold cheek. The form smelled of the river and city streets. It smelled dead. Momentarily confused, the dog swam beside the body for a few yards, before letting it go its way while he went his.

17

"What do you think about when you're practicing law?" Marguerite asked Tubby.

"What do you mean?" he asked. He was sitting at the room's small round table looking at the dark through a crack in the curtain.

"I'm just keeping the conversation going," she said.

Tubby pushed the curtains closed and swung around to look at her.

"I try to imagine a place where it's always safe and warm. What do you think about when you're keeping track of the market in pork bellies?" He had learned that Marguerite worked for a commodities broker.

"I think about going on a nice vacation." She was on her stomach on top of the bed sampling macadamia nuts from a can she'd found in the mini-bar.

"Where else have you gone?" he asked.

"Oh, I went to Disney World one time, and there was a heat wave. And I've been to Cancún, but there was a hurricane and we had to go back to Mexico City, which I didn't like. And then I came to Mardi Gras and it flooded."

"You're no stranger to natural disasters then."

"Well, I haven't had an earthquake yet, or a volcano, but I wouldn't be surprised if that was in store for me next year."

The telephone beeped softly, and Tubby jumped up to answer it.

"Yes?"

"Room service, sir. You asked us to call when we had the kitchen up again."

"Oh, yes," Tubby said brightly.

"I must tell you that the chef has abandoned the regular menu. Tonight he is serving the following: as an appetizer, Crabmeat Imperial with Roasted Pecans, or shrimp fritters. For a soup we have a simple corn and potato, or a rich oyster and artichoke. For salad, we are serving only Boston lettuce with pieces of walnuts. Our entrées are Oysters en Brochette with Mushroom Caps and Bacon, herbed chicken, or angel-hair pasta with a very light crawfish sauce. And the fish of the day is redfish."

"Incredible," Tubby exhaled. He put his hand over the mouthpiece. "The cook is cleaning out the kitchen. We get *tout le bataclan*."

Not familiar with that dish, Marguerite just raised her eyebrows.

"There are two of us," Tubby said. "We'll take both of the appetizers, both of the soups, two salads, the oysters en brochette, and the chicken. You like pasta?" he asked Marguerite.

She nodded.

"And the pasta too," Tubby concluded. "Do you have wine?"

"Of course. May I recommend a bottle of the Loire Valley Clos de Varenne Savennières to start, or the Château Val Joanis, 1997, from the Côtes du Lubéron with your meal?"

"That would be just fine."

"Both?"

"Yes, please."

"Excellent, sir. Will that be all?"

"What else have you got?"

"We have some very wonderful strawberries, and they must be eaten. We have no way to keep them cool. Would you like a bowl?"

"Yes, I believe we would." Tubby hung up and sank back in his chair, worn out.

"A good meal?" Marguerite asked.

"It might be fantastic. They're cooking everything they've got."

"How long do you think it'll take to get here?"

"I didn't ask."

She put the plastic cap back on her macadamias. She rolled over onto her back and raised one long leg to look at her toes. "What do we do while we wait?" she asked aloud.

Tubby studied her pale smooth ankle.

"Let's watch a movie," he said, reaching for the remote on the nightstand.

It turned out that the only one they hadn't seen was *Penelope's Secret,* for adults only.

"Let's give it a try. Might learn something," Marguerite said to herself, pressing buttons.

"You like naughty films?" she asked Tubby.

"Some are better than others," he said. He really was not very well versed in this area.

The screen filled up with a man and a woman making love in a field of flowers on a hillside in France.

"Those black boots you wear are very strange-looking," Marguerite commented.

Tubby laughed.

"And they're too tight," he said. "I'd take 'em off, but I don't know if I can."

"I might help you in a minute," she said absently, engrossed in what was happening on screen. "How about a refill?" She waved her cup in the air.

"At your service," Tubby said, rising to the occasion.

"Ta-da!" Wendell sang as he proudly set his steaming bowl of gumbo on the table. He had lit the candles and gotten Big Top and Monk seated. Rue was still in the bedroom, but his place was set with a knife, fork, and napkin.

"This is a very special Creole delicacy, created by a very high Georgia peach," he said, standing back with clasped hands to admire his handiwork.

Monk and Big Top had both washed up and were outfitted in dry shorts from Edward's suitcase. They both went "Mmmm" in appreciation. Monk had a splendid gold Rolex on his wrist. Big Top was wearing a gaudy diamond necklace. He secretly thought he might give it to Monk when they got back to their house trailer in Wiggins. Their misgivings about

Rue and the fate of their mission had been partially laid to rest by these tokens.

Wendell crossed the room and tapped on the bedroom door.

"Won't you sit down, Mr. Rue?" he called.

LaRue tried to resist the invitation, but the food smelled so good that he emerged from the back of the house. Sidling over to the table, he joined the party.

"Will you do the honors," Wendell asked Edward, handing him a new bottle of wine. "And I'll make the plates."

He put a big spoonful of rice into each bowl and ladled the gumbo over it. Steam rose from the table. He passed around a crisp loaf of French bread. "Now in just a minute I'll bring out the main course," he announced.

"We don't usually eat like this on a job," Big Top said.

Monk tasted his soup. "We don't ever eat this good," he said.

"What kind of a job was it?" Edward inquired.

The three robbers all ignored him.

"I think this is such fun," Wendell said on his way back to the kitchen. "I have a pecan pie for dessert."

The cart that rolled through the door of room 209 was covered with silver serving dishes.

Tubby had to flip on the light in the compact entry hall so that the waiter could see which way to push.

"I'm short of cash," Tubby said.

"That's all right, sir," the uniformed attendant said, feeling an affinity for Tubby's red toreador pants. "You can sign the back of the check and indicate your tip, and they'll cash it for me at the bar."

"That's cool," Tubby said, and scribbled.

He wheeled the tray the rest of the way into the bedroom himself. The only light came from the flickering television set.

"Let's spread it all out," he suggested.

"I want the strawberries now," Marguerite said dreamily.

"What we have here is a feast."

She pressed the mute button and rolled over to see what lay hidden beneath the silver lids.

"Now we won't know how the movie comes out," Tubby complained. The back of a woman's head filled the screen. She was pumping relentlessly on something fleshy.

Marguerite raised her eyebrows.

"That was a joke," he said. "I think we should begin with the Savennières." He fondled the dark green bottle lovingly and used the point of the corkscrew to peel back the foil. "We can sit at the table if you like."

"I'm comfortable here," she said.

"Suit yourself." He took a warm loaf of French bread, the shrimp fritters, and the artichoke soup with him and sat down in one of the chairs.

Marguerite ate a strawberry. "You're looking at me," she said.

"You make such a pretty picture," he said. "Sort of like an oil painting."

She extended one of her legs and admired her toes.

"I'm too hungry to pose," she said, and sat up. She joined Tubby at the table.

He offered her soup and poured them each a glass of wine.

"Are you very successful at what you do?" she asked.

"I try to be," he replied.

"Are you married? I suppose I should have asked you that before I let you into my room."

"I'm divorced. Is that the right answer?"

"Children?"

"Three—all girls. The youngest is a sophomore in high school. The oldest goes to Sophie Newcomb. How about you?"

"I was married once, when I was nineteen. It was a big mistake, and it only lasted two years."

"No kids?"

"No, thank God."

Tubby tested the Boston lettuce salad with the pieces of walnuts.

"You like your kids?" she asked him.

"Yes, very much. I try to stay involved with their lives."

"That's a nice thing to say."

"I didn't mean it to sound nice. I've caused a lot of disruptions for them. But I suppose change is what life's all about. They're different people every week, it seems. I'm just trying to remain relevant."

"Well, I think it's nice that fathers care about their daughters. Mine wanted to, but he never understood how."

"Where is he now?"

"He passed away last year."

"I'm sorry to hear that."

"It's okay. You ever want to have more kids?"

"I guess I'm open to the possibility, if I ever, uh . . ." He shrugged.

"I know, met the right woman. You still love your wife?"

"Dining alone with a beautiful woman in a four-star hotel, I'd be a fool to say yes."

She fluttered her eyelashes at him. "I'm not looking for compliments, you know."

"Of course not. You don't need to."

"Are you flirting with me?"

Tubby smiled at her across the Crabmeat Imperial. Over her shoulder, the couple on the silent screen had reversed positions. The woman's eyes were closed and her mouth was hanging open and repeating some word over and over again while she rocked back and forth.

"Well, it's okay if you are," Marguerite said. "I guess I came to New Orleans to be flirted with."

"I'm out of practice," Tubby said.

"Me too, to tell you the truth. I've discovered that life without men can be very peaceful."

"What do you like to do for fun, when you're back home?" he asked.

"I don't like to go to the movies," Marguerite replied.

"Really? I don't either." Tubby was surprised.

"I love to get away from the city. Sometimes a friend takes me out in his boat on Lake Michigan."

"I've got a boat. I take it out on Lake Pontchartrain or

into the marshes. They're very pretty. Maybe you'd like to go while you're here."

"Haven't you noticed, it's flooding?"

"Oh, yeah. I forgot. You ever go fishing?"

"A few times. I had fun."

"I like to fish," Tubby said. He was thinking that Jynx Margolis, the woman he sometimes went out with, answered all these questions wrong.

"I know this will sound funny," Marguerite said, "but I've got a motorcycle. It's just a little Suzuki. I look forward to summers just so I can ride it. Not very adult, huh?"

"You gotta be kidding! I have a motorcycle. It's a Harley Hydra Glide."

"No way. You?"

"What do you mean, me?"

"A lawyer and everything?"

"Just because I'm a lawyer doesn't mean I don't get a charge when that baby goes 'Brmmm, brmmm.'" Tubby twisted an imaginary throttle with his fist. "I live to ride."

Marguerite rested her fork on her lower lip and smiled at him.

"You just might do," she said.

"Do what?" he asked, but he was thinking that this relationship might be going somewhere.

"Now, what I want you to do," LaRue instructed Big Top, "is to tie up these two assholes with their hands behind their backs. Then tie their feet together. Then put them on the floor, back to back, and tie them to each other. Then you and Monk can sleep on the couch or the chair, whatever you like, but be sure they don't get loose."

All of those mentioned, who had been finishing up great slices of pecan pie, stared at him.

"I enjoyed the supper," LaRue said. "Anyone wants the rest of my pie can have it."

He shoved his chair back from the table and stood up.

"There's no need to do that," Edward protested. "We aren't going anywhere."

"You're right about that," LaRue said. "Monk, while Big Top's tying them up, you come on back to the bedroom with me and we'll talk about getting out of here tomorrow, rain or shine. Then you can explain it to Big Top."

"What about the dishes?" Wendell asked, horrified by the prospect of spending the night trussed up.

LaRue bent over and slapped Wendell hard across the mouth.

"I've been meaning to do that since I got here," he told his shocked victim. "You can save 'em till morning or do 'em now, whatever you please, sweetheart."

18

It was Fat Tuesday.

Tubby pulled the curtain aside to see what Mardi Gras morning had brought.

Hallelujah! For the moment it was not raining, but it had been recently and looked like it would be again soon. He put on the soft white bathrobe the hotel provided and slid the glass doors aside to stand on the balcony.

It was early, not much after six o'clock, and somewhere the sun was up. But in the old city of New Orleans a light cottony fog hung low over the buildings.

There was standing water in the gutters, and the street and sidewalks were layered with debris. Bits of plastic, plant life, latex, and paper had been blended together into a single odoriferous stew, which was deposited in crusty swirls wherever the water had receded.

Shopkeepers and club bouncers were beginning to venture into the street, assessing the damage and checking the sky for another onslaught. A slender brown woman in a tight black cocktail dress and high heels walked rapidly alone through the center of them all in the direction of Jackson Square. She disappeared in the mist.

He heard the TV behind him, deeply inhaled the morning, and withdrew through the curtains. Marguerite had the local news on. She was propped up in bed, eating an apple.

"Police Chief Pendleton said at a news conference that concluded just a few minutes ago that he has canceled, repeat, canceled, the Zulu and Rex parades due to the extremely dangerous weather conditions throughout the city. Citing the flooding of numerous streets and neighborhoods, the power outages affecting much of our area, high winds, and the need for emergency vehicles to get through, the chief, after consulting with the mayor, has canceled the Zulu and Rex parades. No word yet on the Elks or the Crescent City Truck parades.

"We do understand that arrangements are being made to transport Rex to City Hall where he will receive the keys to our very wet city from the mayor. Later he will travel to the Hilton Hotel, by boat or helicopter if necessary, to join his Queen. Some of the most severe flooding has been reported in the vicinity of that hotel and on downtown streets."

"Dick, have they figured out how the Queen of Comus and her court are getting to the hotel?"

"They say they're working on it, Stephanie. The idea of using a barge has been discussed."

"What are the most severe conditions, as you are hearing about them at City Hall?"

"Apparently, Stephanie, though this has not been confirmed, Melpomene Pumping Station Number One at Broad and Jackson Avenue failed to function most of the night, further aggravating an overflow situation and contributing to the unprecedented flooding of the French Quarter. Reports that the operators of that station were asleep last night during the worst of the rainfall have been denied by Sewerage and Water Board officials. We've got flooding into houses in parts of Uptown, Desire, Lakeview, you name it, it's general, it's all over town. It's all over this part of the state, actually. Plaquemines Parish is under water. But to repeat the main news, just a few minutes ago Chief Pendleton announced that he has canceled both the Zulu and the Rex parades . . ."

Marguerite slid out of bed, her nightgown opening to expose a slice of milk-white skin, for his benefit, he liked to think.

"I have a headache," she said, and wandered into the bathroom. Tubby listened to her brushing her teeth and splashing water around.

"I feel just fine," he said to himself. He opened up one of the cans of orange juice in the miniature icebox and went back outside to stand on the balcony.

A ragtag army of paraders in colorful costumes and pointy hats was working its way down the street toward him. They were tossing out a few trinkets and trying to carry the tune of "It's Carnival Time" on assorted wind instruments and drums.

"It's the Half-Fast Marching Club!" Tubby yelled through the curtains. "Marguerite, come quick. It's a Mardi Gras parade!"

"Hey, Pete! Hey, Pete! Hey, Pete!" Tubby was jumping

up and down and waving his arms. "Throw me something! Hey, Pete!" Marguerite, coming out of the bathroom, thought he was nuts.

A couple of the guys in the parade noticed them and fired gobs of beads at the balcony. Marguerite ducked, and Tubby grabbed a handful just before they hit her head. When she opened her eyes a bouquet of red silk roses landed in her hand.

"Oh, this is fun," she said.

The merry band continued up the street toward a bar that was opening its doors just for them. Their music stuck around after they were out of sight.

"Now what?" Marguerite asked, headache gone. She fixed the roses in her hair.

"I don't know. That may be it for Mardi Gras." He put an arm around her waist and they bumped hips.

"I guess we ought to be thinking about breakfast," he said.

"You're right. Sex is good, but let's get down to basics."

The hotel dining room was down to crackers and coffee. No more eggs. No more milk. No more refrigeration.

It had been a long night for Edward and Wendell. One might expect to encounter many hassles traveling through the South, but being tied up on a hard wooden floor, rug or no rug, was not one of them.

Big Top had been grateful enough for Wendell's cooking to leave the knots loose so that slight adjustments in position were possible. Then he had lain down on the couch and hiccuped for the rest of the night.

Monk, trying to get comfortable in his chair, told him to shut up, and Big Top burped. They started laughing.

"Oh, brother, we're back in high school," Edward whispered to Wendell, whose head was resting on his shoulder. They squeezed each other's tethered hands, homesick and miserable together at boys' camp.

"Brrrp," chortled Monk.

"Phhbbp," Big Top cackled. "Hic."

The sound of a bass drum booming right outside the door woke everybody up.

Big Top covered his head with a pillow and turned over on the sofa.

"Damn!" Monk stumbled out of his easy chair and stepped over the tangled legs on the floor to crack open the shutters.

He grinned and started tapping his foot exaggeratedly.

"Bunch of drunks with umbrellas dancin' in the street," he reported, and closed the shutters.

"Oh, please, I need to go," Wendell begged.

Unmoved, Monk went to the bathroom and latched the door behind him.

"Big Top. My man. Let us up," Wendell pleaded.

"Be quiet and leave me alone or you'll be tied up all day," Big Top groaned.

"This is outrageous," Wendell said.

"My back is killing me," Edward said.

"I wish we had gone when you wanted to escape yesterday."

"You had to finish cooking your jambalaya, or whatever it's called."

"Soufflé, baby, and I never expected this." He jerked his wrists.

"Quit that! You're making the rope cut right into my skin."

"I'm sorry. I'm just getting frustrated. And I need to go to the BATHROOM!"

"Help," Edward said softly.

The bedroom door slammed open and Rue stuck his skinny head out, checking his surroundings.

"Big Top, where's Monk?" he asked loudly.

"In the bathroom," Big Top said through the pillow.

"How are you boys doing?" Rue asked the anguished pair tied together on the floor.

"Just like you'd imagine," Edward said.

"Worse than that," Wendell said. "Can you please release us now." His tone was sort of surly.

"Sure," Rue said. Clad in Wendell's bathrobe, he went into the kitchen and returned with a carving knife.

"Don't twitch on me or you might lose an artery," he said, sliding the knife between their wrists and starting to saw.

"I'd let you untie your own feet, but you might not have the smarts for it," he said pleasantly, and freed their ankles.

The two men rolled apart, and in their private worlds began massaging their extremities.

There was a loud flush, and Monk emerged from the bathroom.

"Next," he proclaimed, scratching the curly black hair on his mahogany-colored chest. "What's for breakfast?"

"Ask Wendell," LaRue said. "He's the cook."

Breakfast, it turned out, was yesterday's French bread and some old fig preserves from a dusty, but sealed and ribboned, jar found next to the last of the dish towels. This was consumed quickly and it became apparent that additional provisions would be necessary to get them through the morning. It would be the middle of the afternoon, LaRue told them, before they would be leaving.

"There's a Popeye's up on Canal Street," Big Top said. "I know that much. If anybody's open, they will be."

"If it's not, one of those raghead stores on Bourbon Street has gotta be," Monk said. "I know they'll have candy bars and nuts. Maybe a sandwich."

"I'll go," Big Top offered, running his fingers through his lopsided red hair.

"You reckon you can find your way back?" LaRue asked.

"That's a bad habit. Thinking everybody's stupid," Big Top told him.

"Now, now. Don't be sensitive," LaRue told him.

"For all you guys know, I could be a genius-level."

"Don't push it," Monk said. "Who's got any cash for this mission?"

"What about from the bank?" Big Top asked.

"You're not too stupid, are you, Big Top," LaRue said.

"That stuff may be hot. C'mon, ante up whoever wants something."

His two confederates went to look for some money in their old pants, and Edward went to get his wallet out of his jacket hanging in the closet behind the bathroom door. He pulled out a twenty, but LaRue followed him and confiscated the wallet. He appropriated the rest of the bills, stuffed them into his pocket, and handed the wallet back to Edward.

"Okay, Big Top, see what you can do," Rue said. "And if you find anything hot to eat, grab two."

Wearing his borrowed shorts and sneakers, Big Top ventured out into the wet street.

"Hey, someone swiped our canoe!" he exclaimed.

"Fuckin' city," Monk swore.

Uncertain about exactly where Canal Street was, Big Top set off down the foggy byway.

19

Morning came to Calhoun Street, bringing scattered showers and an off-key trumpet call from the front porch of the Brownlee residence.

Collette curled her legs underneath her and sat up sleepy-eyed on the couch with a blanket wrapped around her shoulders.

Bradley was snoring on a pallet spread on the floor. Mr. Brownlee was standing in the front door, looking out, and Junior was heralding Mardi Gras on his golden band bugle. He was outfitted in his red and white Cohen High School marching band uniform, except he was barefoot.

"Good morning," Collette said to Mr. Brownlee.

"Good morning to you," he said. "We'll have you some breakfast in just a little bit. I think the bathroom is free if you want to try to slip in now."

"Thanks," she said. "Is Junior marching in a parade today?"

"He thinks he is." Noah chuckled. "I don't believe there're going to be any parades today."

Collette stepped over Bradley to look outside through the

screen. The street remained a long brown river. The water might have come down a few inches, but the bottom step to the porch was still submerged. Junior's trumpet rang through the neighborhood.

The White Cloud Cadillac still blocked the street, water to its door handles.

"Where's the cabdriver?" Collette asked.

"He's gone," Mr. Brownlee said. "He must have swum away."

Across the canal a door opened and another kid with a Cohen uniform backed out, a snare drum strapped to his waist. With a wave at Junior he joined in and picked up the beat. Carnival was beginning.

While Collette and Bradley polished off scrambled eggs and toast, Mr. Brownlee located a flat-bottomed fiberglass bass boat, colored dull gray. He offered to row Collette home. Bradley lived in Lakeview, but Collette invited him to make her home the next stop on his journey.

Little kids had begun playing on the roof of the White Cloud when the three of them climbed aboard the boat and pushed off from the porch. Mr. Brownlee had a canoe paddle and Collette and Bradley both had poles fashioned out of wooden curtain rods.

Several other instruments—a saxophone, a clarinet, and a trombone—had joined the front porch concert by then. There was a battle of the bands going on, with Kennedy, A. B. Bell, and McDonough 38 represented. A young girl was twirling a baton on one stoop, and next door to her two others were high-stepping and acting hot.

Brownlee grinned and waved. "Happy Mardi Gras," he called to the kids.

Bradley, who had not contributed much to the conversation at the Brownlees', turned out to be an enthusiastic poleman. While Mr. Brownlee paddled smoothly in the back of the boat, Bradley took mighty stabs at the muck with his stick. He stripped off his shirt and Collette, in the middle, thought he looked pretty good. She had already classified him as a "man with a bad attitude," but she was thinking about giving him a second chance.

"Garbage can ahead," Bradley cried happily. Stroke, stroke. "Here come some two-by-fours."

They made a graceful turn onto Freret Street and sailed into a flotilla of bare-chested black men with Afro fright wigs, floating on inflated inner tubes. One dangled a silver-painted coconut tantalizingly before Collette's eyes.

"Oh, Zulu coconut! Please, mister," she screamed. At the last possible moment, before the tube drifted out of the reach of the occupants of the bass boat, the white-lipped savage pressed the prize into the young girl's wriggling fingers.

"Hey, coconut," Bradley called, after the waterborne contingent of the famous social aid and pleasure club passed, but he was miles too late.

"Nah-nah-nah-nah-nah, " Collette taunted.

"Damn," Bradley said, jealous. "Hey, here comes another boat." He pointed.

"It's an Indian," Mr. Brownlee said, voice full of appreciation.

Indeed, a chief approached in a pirogue carefully paddled

by a young boy in cutoff jeans. The chief faced rearward in his boat, relying on his aide to see and avoid any obstacles, and his opulent headdress was fully displayed. It was a soft, creamy, symmetrical array of purple, red, blue, yellow, and black plumage, fully a yard high, and it confronted them as if several peacocks, posed together, were spreading their feathers all at once.

"It's beautiful," Collette said in awe.

"Hey, Chief," Bradley shouted as the two boats passed, but the Indian would not look their way.

"Looking good, Samuel," Mr. Brownlee said, and the Indian turned and gave his neighbor a small dignified nod.

"I've never seen a Mardi Gras Indian before," Collette said, watching the pirogue slip away with its dazzling passenger. "I've lived here all my life, but I've never actually seen one."

"There's a few around here," Mr. Brownlee said. "I guess he's going to join up with the rest of 'em downtown."

"What can they do in all this water?" Bradley asked.

"They'll do something," Mr. Brownlee said. "It wouldn't be Mardi Gras without the Indians dancing, and a little water ain't gonna stop their Mardi Gras."

"I don't think they'll be having any parades today," Collette said.

"That's probably true," Mr. Brownlee said, "but the old traditions get carried on."

"As long as they're important to people, I suppose they will be," Collette said.

They entered her neighborhood, where the houses were bigger but the water was just as deep.

"Look straight ahead and pretend you don't see the homes, and it's just like being in the swamp," she said to Bradley.

"Yeah, it really could be, with all these trees standing in the water."

Except for a few abandoned vehicles, their roofs poking above the surface like colorful islands, all of the cars were crammed together on people's lawns and driveways, where some were escaping the water. Most of them, however, would have soaked brakes and rank carpets.

"That's my house." Collette pointed.

Mr. Brownlee steered the boat to the iron picket fence, and Bradley opened the gate so they could float up the walk to the front steps. The boat made contact with a loud crunch. Bradley grabbed the huge clay pot where once an azalea had lived and hung on for dear life while Collette crawled out. When she had her legs underneath her, she took Bradley's arm and helped him ashore.

"I don't know how to thank you, Mr. Brownlee," she said, and gave him her hand to shake. In her other she gripped her silver coconut tightly.

"Glad to help y'all kids," he replied. "You weren't any trouble."

"Yeah, uh, thanks," Bradley said, and extended his hand as well.

Studying the boy from beneath his thick eyebrows, Mr. Brownlee took the hand and shook it.

"And please tell Mrs. Brownlee thanks for all the wonderful food," Collette said happily. "I really had a good time."

"Can we pay you?" Bradley asked.

Brownlee pushed off the steps and drifted into the yard, not bothering to answer.

"Thank you." Collette waved as he paddled out to the street. He returned the wave and started toward his home.

"I guess he didn't want money," Bradley said.

"You are really dumb," Collette told him bluntly. "I wonder if I have my keys." She stuck her fingers in the miniature pack Velcroed to her shorts.

"I sure didn't expect to spend so much of Mardi Gras without drinking a beer," Bradley complained.

Collette found her key.

"Don't worry," she said. "My mom will probably offer you one. All I want is a bath."

20

"No more room service," Tubby said sadly, resting the phone in its cradle.

"What did they suggest we do?" Marguerite asked, drying her hair.

"They just apologized. The kitchen's closed until they get it cleaned up. They hope to be serving by this afternoon, if it doesn't start raining again."

"I bet there's someplace open nearby. I'm getting stir-crazy in this room anyhow."

"Okay. Get dressed and we'll go exploring. I'd like to check on my car, too, if the streets are open. We might even be able to drive out of here."

It took Marguerite a long time, by Tubby's standards, to get ready. She was finding it difficult to select the appropriate attire for scattered showers and standing water. She owned ragged corduroys and galoshes back home, but she had not thought to bring those with her to Mardi Gras. Finally she settled on her new Calvin Klein jeans, a tangerine polo shirt, and her new Reeboks. Tubby, meanwhile, watched Nash Roberts explain that Claiborne Avenue was still submerged, along with large portions of Nashville, Jefferson, and Napoleon Avenues. So much for driving home. The aerial footage of car roofs floating like lily pads on familiar streets and vehicles of all sorts mired in sticky mud on the neutral grounds was entertaining. A lot of the Calliope and C. J. Peete projects were inundated, and the Red Cross was trying to move some sick people off the roofs by helicopter. Human remains had been sighted, but not confirmed, in floodwaters. Tubby shuddered, thinking about his unfortunate client. He also wondered whether there might be any reappearance of the remains of his former law partner, Reggie Turntide.

"I guess we can't drive anywhere," he told Marguerite.

"Then let's walk," she said, checking her rear in the mirror.

They took the stairs.

Tubby spotted Dan in the lobby. He was carrying someone's luggage into the elevator, and didn't see Tubby when he waved.

The crowd from the previous night had thinned out considerably, but there were still a few crumpled travelers sprawled on the chairs and sofas, sleeping or staring around with glazed expressions on their faces.

In the great outdoors, the world was wet, but the streets were clear.

Lots of people were busy sweeping water and all manner of glop out of their vestibules and swapping stories of survival.

The absence of parades and the sudden blasts of rain were no deterrents to quite a few determined revelers. It was, after all, Mardi Gras, and the tradition was to drink all day and costume, copulate, or capsize. Accordingly, there were spirited citizens outfitted as ducks, scuba divers, and sharks. There were skimpy bikinis, on man and woman. The less adventurous, oddly dressed as normal people, gasped and laughed at bare chests and black rubber wet suits. Not to mention nude women and green frog men.

From out of the swamp, a people's Mardi Gras was arising to reclaim the city.

Up the street came a somewhat organized marching parade. Tubby recognized the men, dressed variously in women's gowns, complete with rouge, tuxedos, derby hats, and black short pants, as the Jefferson City Buzzards.

"They've made every Mardi Gras for a hundred years," Tubby yelled at Marguerite with unconcealed exuberance. "Way to go, guys!"

The Buzzards had a bass drum and a couple of trumpets. They made a lot of noise and tried to trade long beads for kisses with any female who came too close.

Marguerite was a novice and thus got caught in a beery embrace. She was immediately appeased by a three-foot strand of pearls.

"Happy Gras, honey," the Buzzard said contentedly, and marched on.

She had to fumble in her shirt to get her bra readjusted.

"Rather fresh," she said.

A fat bald man with the mashed stub of a cigar stuck in his teeth was throwing piles of wet magazines and newspapers over the curb.

"Hey, Nick," Tubby called.

"It's Tubby." The squat man straightened up. "Howya makin' out?"

"Okay, I guess. Wet. This is my friend, Marguerite . . . uh . . ."

"Patino," she supplied.

"Right," Tubby continued. "Marguerite, this is Nick the Newsman. We're walking on his street. You had a lot of damage, Nick?"

"Oh, yeah, lots of magazines and all my newspapers, just about. That's a bunch of crap. My display racks are all full of this shit, or whatever you call it. My juice is out. My little dog I keep here pissed all over the cash register. But I guess I'll make out."

"Listen, Nick, do you have any idea where there's something for breakfast around here?"

"I heard Popeye's might be open up on Canal. Everything else is closed up, I think. I got some ham salad in the back if you want to try that. It's kind of old."

He unplugged the cigar long enough to spit into a puddle.

"Hey, check that out." Nick nodded toward the street where two big-busted figures, nude but for black panties and garters, strolled hand in hand down the lane.

"You wanna make a bet they's guys or dolls?" Nick asked, and coughed out a laugh around the sweet potato in his mouth.

Marguerite's mouth was open and her eyes were big.

"Look around, dearie, and you will see things you've never imagined before," Tubby murmured in her ear, and goosed her a little bit in the back of her tangerine shirt.

And walking right behind the brazen nudes was one of the men who had killed Tubby's client.

"That's the guy in the canoe." Tubby grabbed Marguerite's arm and pointed to the tall gangling man in Bermuda shorts sauntering along Royal Street, eyeballing the strange crowd and carrying an immense sack of fried chicken.

Raindrops fell for a few seconds, causing a ripple of pained groans along the street that stopped just as abruptly as the shower did.

"He's the one who shot the lady?" Marguerite asked excitedly.

"No, but he was in the boat. He couldn't have been more than six feet away from me. I'm sure it's him." Tubby was looking around for a cop.

"He's getting away," Marguerite hissed in his ear.

"Nick, you see that guy with the red hair and the chicken?"

"Yeah."

"Him and these two other guys shot a lady I was with yesterday during the flood. And killed her."

Nick's eyes lit up. He liked crime. Thus, in New Orleans, he was often happy. He started chewing his cigar.

"Damn," Tubby said. "Where's the cops when you need them?"

"Pulling drowned people out of cars, is what I hear," Nick said. "Or carrying the politicians over the puddles so they won't get their little feetsies wet."

Big Top was disappearing.

"Hell, I've got to follow him. Do me a favor, will you,

Nick? At the Royal Montpelier there's a bellhop, Dan. He's my good friend. Lock up your store just a minute. Go get Dan and tell him what I'm doing and which way I went. Tell him to come looking for me."

"Okay." Nick was ready.

"I'm coming," Marguerite said.

"Suit yourself," Tubby said.

Regretting that they had not eaten, Tubby and Marguerite trailed Big Top down Royal Street, wading through the deep water at St. Ann, threading single file along the one dry sidewalk on Dumaine, trying to keep the head of Panama Red in sight.

The crowd thinned out some as they went along, making concealment next to impossible. Big Top, however, did not detect his furtive pursuers because he was now eating a thigh one-handed and was otherwise oblivious to his surroundings.

They were half a block behind him, sloshing through a shallow, fast-running freshet covering the pavement, when their quarry disappeared around the corner. By the time Tubby and Marguerite poked their heads around he was no longer in sight.

"Stay here," Tubby ordered, and he tiptoed cautiously down the sidewalk looking for the open door.

"Oooh," Marguerite screamed.

Tubby looked back to see her being prodded forcibly forward by a short, muscular black man, also wearing shorts, whom he recognized as being one of yesterday's executioners.

"Looking for something, dude?" the man demanded sternly.

"No, and take your hands off that woman," Tubby croaked.

The man seemed to find that funny. Keeping one meaty hand clamped on Marguerite's small bicep, which Tubby knew to be soft and freckled, and without taking a step, the man jammed the barrel of a large handgun into the lawyer's stomach. Tubby was caught so suddenly he nearly doubled over. He also stumbled backwards, and kept backing up until he tripped over some stone steps and sat down on them hard.

Monk rapped on the green shutters with his pistol without loosening his grip on the girl. The door opened, and Big Top stuck his head out.

"Look who was following you," Monk jeered, prodding the woman and gesturing with his pistol at Tubby.

Big Top wiped the chicken grease off his chin.

Then he was pushed aside by LaRue, who needed only one quick look at the trio outside to comprehend the situation.

"Bring 'em in quick," he said. "And keep that gun out of sight."

Tubby lunged for the legs of the man holding Marguerite and was rewarded with a solid thunk on the side of his head with the butt of the pistol.

A hand grabbed his hair, another hooked under his arms, and he was agonizingly dragged into the apartment and slammed onto the floor.

Some thinly clad girls in a seaweed-draped funny car driven by a man dressed like a crawfish waved at them, but getting no response, kept on going.

● ● ●

"So what do we have here?" LaRue inquired, after he had frisked Tubby thoroughly, relieved him of his Gold Master-Card, and made him sit on the muddy floor.

Marguerite had also been pushed roughly to the rug near the couch at the other side of the room, and Monk and Big Top were swaggering around her. Tubby rubbed the side of his head where the blow from the pistol had raised a tender egg.

"It says on the credit card 'Attorney-at-Law,'" Rue continued. "That you?" He hunkered down to be at eye level with Tubby.

Tubby nodded.

LaRue toyed with the trainman's watch he had lifted from Tubby's pants. He stuck it in his pocket with a malicious grin.

"You're dressed kind of cute for a lawyer," he said, dissing Tubby's red pants.

His victim was too embarrassed to respond.

"And you, young lady. What about you?" LaRue refocused his lizard-like eyes.

"I'm an executive assistant," she said. "From Chicago."

"Executive assistant, huh?" LaRue asked conversationally. "What are you doing here?"

Marguerite sat up and leaned against the couch. "I'm just visiting town for Mardi Gras."

"Why were you following my friend?"

"I wasn't."

LaRue pulled on one pink ear and nodded, as if he understood.

"We've met before," he said, turning to the attorney-at-law. Tubby wrinkled his brow. "No, I don't think so."

"Yeah, we have. And you do think so." LaRue stood up. "Monk, use the rest of that cord I cut off our cook and let's tie these two up until we decide what to do with them."

"Bullshit!" Tubby roared, rising off the floor.

Rue smacked him on the forehead again with the side of the pistol, this time so hard that Tubby blacked out for an instant, crashed against the wall, and fell to his knees seeing stars. He wanted to die but couldn't.

When Big Top started tying knots, he didn't offer much resistance.

"Now you, young lady. What's your story?"

"Honest, I'm just a tourist. I just met this man. We were taking a walk together."

LaRue stood over her shaking his head. Then he reached down, put his hand around her throat, and slowly lifted her up. She was too frightened to react.

Switching his grip to the back of her neck, LaRue forced her toward the bedroom.

"I think we can get to the truth," he said.

"Hey, Rue," Monk said from where he was helping to truss Tubby up.

"What?" LaRue looked back, keeping his hand fastened on the woman.

"If you mess with the girl, I'm out of here." Monk stood up.

"What the fuck are you giving me?" LaRue growled.

"I ain't in this to mess with no women. I wasn't raised that way."

Rue let go of Marguerite and swung around to face Monk.

"You weren't fuckin' raised that way. Who the fuck do you think you are, jailbait?"

Monk didn't back up, but he was trembling a little.

"I ain't telling you what to do, Rue. I just didn't sign up for no rape. That girl didn't do nothing to us. You do anything to her, I'm gone."

LaRue bared his teeth like a rat getting ready to bite. Then he made a horrible grin out of it.

He reached behind him without looking and grabbed a piece of Marguerite, then threw her across the room at Monk, sending both of them sprawling into a chair.

"You're a dumb fuck, Monk," he said, "but I ain't ready to lose you yet."

LaRue took one quick step and kicked Tubby under the belt. It made him feel better.

Nick had no trouble finding Dan at the Royal Montpelier.

"Dude work here named Dan Haywood?" he asked the first hotel employee he encountered. He was directed toward a bearlike man overflowing a bellhop's uniform, who at the moment was gesturing wildly to a tall black woman wearing a purple scarf tied around her hair, a tight sleeveless white top, and khaki slacks, who looked like she was ready to go for a stroll down the boardwalk in Bimini.

Nick rushed over and tugged the big man's sleeve.

"Look, you're a friend of Tubby Dubonnet's?" he asked through the stub of his cigar.

"I am," Dan admitted.

"He asked me to come and get you. He's following this guy shot somebody," Nick said excitedly with the free side of his mouth.

"Which way did he go?" the lady asked, as if it were her business.

"Who're you?" Nick wanted to know.

"I'm a . . ." Detective Fox Lane began.

"She's a friend of Tubby's," Dan interjected. "Where did he go?"

"He and this good-lookin' woman in an ernge shirt went down the street that way not three minutes ago. They was following this carrottop carrying a bag of Popeye's."

"So what am I supposed to do?"

"That's the whole story." Nick looked at the big bellman like he was a side of meat. "He said the guy he was chasing shot somebody and to come get you."

"Let's go after him," Fox said. She didn't wait for a reply, but started jogging down the now crowded street. They noticed she was wearing sneakers.

"Hey, wait!" Dan yelled, and went lumbering after her.

"He's got these red pants on," Nick called. "I'm at the newsstand. Tell me what happens," he said to himself.

21

Bellman Dan and Detective Lane were discovering that searching Royal Street for a man and a woman who were there just a few minutes ago can be a frustrating undertaking. The policewoman moved rapidly through two blocks of puddles and people before pausing to quiz some of the locals mopping up their floors. They tried to remember but shook their heads. Then, in front of an antique shop, a mud-smeared woman said yes, she had seen a man dressed just like a bullfighter and a pretty young Yankee woman edging along the sidewalk and acting peculiar. When Dan staggered up to her, she was pointing down the street in the direction the peculiar pair had gone.

The trail grew cold after that, however, and Fox and Dan circled one block, then another, without result. A sudden downpour cleared the streets and sent the search party scurrying for the shelter of an ornate iron balcony. The shower was over just as suddenly and, like leprechauns popping out from beneath their mushrooms, the flood survivors and merrymakers retook the street.

Fox and Dan made a nuisance of themselves, asking one

lit person after another if any had seen an oddly dressed lawyer and a clean-cut companion. Time passed.

"Any ideas?" Fox asked.

"Not really," Dan said. He was out of his element making like a cop and quizzing strangers. His forte was clandestine intelligence gathering, not interrogating the public. Tubby had appointed Dan to be his rescuer, and he must have had a good reason, but Dan was out of gas.

"I suppose I could go back to the hotel in case he calls." He and the policewoman had slowed to a walk. They were outside a restaurant with a po-boy menu screwed to the wall. The place was locked, but there was a Miller sign glowing in the window.

"We found the body he was talking about, I think," Lane said. "A middle-aged female with a gunshot wound in the head drifted up around Blue Plate Mayonnaise. Some kids found her." Little children were watching them from a second-floor window, their eyes distorted by the wavy glass.

"He was real upset about it," Dan commented, apropos of nothing.

"He was crazy to go off looking for the perps by himself."

"Well, he did have Miss Patino with him."

"You know her?"

"Sure. I introduced them." Just like I introduced Tubby to Mrs. Lostus, he thought. "She's a tourist from up North, where it's cold."

"Oh, great. And suppose she gets hurt. That kind of news the city doesn't need." It disgusted Fox that that was the kind of news the city kept getting.

"How's he know you?" Dan inquired, ready to sit down.

"We were in law school together." Fox kept walking, looking in windows, through gates.

"Really?" Dan said in shock. "I guess you kind of do look like a lawyer though. You've got a gun stuck in the back of your pants."

"You can see it?"

"Yeah."

"I'm a cop more than a lawyer, but I do pay my bar association dues."

"I usually stay away from cops," Dan mentioned.

Lane looked him over and lifted an eyebrow.

"And why is that?" she asked, suspicious.

Dan shrugged. "I do some union work. I guess I can say that because you New Orleans cops have a union."

"Is that what you call it? I'm not that involved." Fox's tone was angry. "What so-called union do you work for?"

"We can talk about that sometime," Dan said evasively. "Is your real name Fox?"

"Short for Foxelle," she said. "C'mon, let's do something."

She had to raise her voice because of the racket coming from a strange vehicle rounding the corner topped with nearly nude dancing girls.

Helplessly lassoed on the floor and slightly groggy, Tubby watched the three robbers make preparations for their exit.

First they ate all the fried chicken. Then the ones who responded to "Big Top" and "Monk" sat at the dining room table and played cards with Marguerite and the two men who evidently lived here. The crooks tried to explain the game of bourré, and the civilians tried to teach everybody bridge. Marguerite eventually got them all playing hearts. The one called "Roux" had disappeared into the bedroom. Tubby felt left out.

"Damn, I got the bad queen," Monk complained.

"He's trying to shoot the moon," Marguerite warned.

"Cut the table talk, please," Edward said.

"How come I'm the only one tied up?" Tubby asked. He was ignored.

"It's your lead, Big Top," Wendell prompted.

"Hello," Tubby said. "Maybe I could at least have something to eat."

"There's a leftover biscuit," Monk said. "Why don't you give it to him?" He pointed at Wendell.

Marguerite was not dealing with the problem at all. She was, in fact, giggling while sorting out her hand.

"I don't think you'd want to eat that, would you?" Wendell asked, picking through his cards and ebulliently slapping down a red jack.

"Hell yes," Tubby said. "I haven't eaten all day."

Reluctantly, Wendell got up and lifted a cold biscuit out of the crumpled greasy paper bag with two fingertips. He bent over Tubby to poke it in his mouth.

"That phone over there," Tubby whispered, pointing with his chin. "Call nine-one-one and tell them we've been kidnapped by murderers. They can trace the call to this address."

Wendell looked worried. He shook his head. "I'm afraid of what they'll do," he said in a low voice.

"Man, I think they're going to kill us anyway."

Wendell shook his head again, rejecting that information. "Eat your biscuit," he said nervously.

Tubby closed his eyes and opened his mouth.

Wendell got tired of waiting for Tubby to swallow, so he left the rest of the biscuit on Tubby's leg and went back to the game.

"It's the Monster," Fox Lane said.

"What is?" Dan asked, startled.

"The guy in the funny car. It's Monster Mudbug."

"I wasn't looking at the guy."

The strange car with gyrating sea clams and naked mermaids on top, a backfiring gas generator, and speakers blaring "Shake Your Booty," was being badly driven by a man dressed as a shiny boiled crawfish.

"He knows Tubby, too," Fox muttered. "That lawyer has a whole zooful of friends."

The car came closer, sucking people onto their balconies and through the doors of cozy barrooms. A crowd of volunteer belly dancers had formed around the open-topped vehicle and was moving slowly down the narrow street, gyrating to the music.

"Those are some pretty good exotic dancers," Dan said.

"It takes a real diehard to be thinking about Mardi Gras after a flood like this," Fox observed.

"Well, I heard on TV that the Moss Man was out in some kind of a special speedboat on Broadway," Dan reported. "You can't keep those serious Mardi Gras people down."

The rolling fiesta was threatening to cram Dan and Fox onto the sidewalk and against the wall of an antique store, but the agile policewoman used something authoritative in her voice to slide through the dancers up to the float and get apace with the driver.

She knocked on the Monster's red plastic carapace and finally got his attention.

"Have you seen Tubby Dubonnet?" she yelled.

The Monster fought to orient himself in space and time and forgot about steering.

"Mr. Tubby?" he shouted, trying to see who he was talking to.

"That's right. I'm Officer Lane. I've heard about you from Tubby. It's important."

"Sure." Monster Mudbug nodded inside his shell. "Where did I see him? It's kind of hard to know exactly what street you're on in here."

His front fenders were grazing the rear of a fat naked man, and Fox Lane pushed the steering wheel a couple of inches to the left.

"It was like he was drunk," the Monster said, struggling to remember. "Two guys were, like, helping him up the steps, like minutes ago."

"Where was this?" Fox yelled.

"I'm thinking." Monster whacked his pointed head with his claw. "Governor Nicholls Street. I'm real sure it was Governor Nicholls Street 'cause it was right after I passed Verti Marte. That next block was where I saw him."

"Okay," Fox shouted. "What door?"

"It's like the second or third place. I'm pretty sure. I thought he waved at me."

A tipsy babe jumped on the front of his funny car and struck a depraved pose so that her friend could take her picture with a tiny yellow camera.

"Hey, get off the Monster Mobile," the boss cried. "I can't see."

The vehicle plowed through the crowd, leaving just one spectator jumping around holding her ankle, and gradually straightened course.

Fox held her position until all the commotion washed past her. Just as Dan was stepping off the curb to join her, she set off running in the direction of Governor Nicholls Street. He wheezed and thumped in pursuit, trying not to lose his Foreign Legionnaire's hat.

22

In Lafitte's Lair, the telephone beside the couch rang once, suspending the conversation at the card table.

"Rue must've got it in the bedroom," Big Top concluded when it didn't ring again.

"It's your deal, Marguerite," Monk said, tossing the cards over to her. "Who's ahead?"

The bedroom door creaked open, and LaRue stepped out.

"We're going to be leaving in a few minutes," he said. He told Monk and Big Top to get their stuff together.

"What about all these people?" Monk asked.

"We'll deal with that next." He looked down at Tubby. "Where's your car?"

"Under water about five miles from here," Tubby lied.

"I'd like your opinion on a few things," LaRue told him.

"Yeah? Like what?"

"Why don't you tell everybody what's the penalty for kidnapping in this state?"

"Could be up to life at hard labor at Angola Prison Farm," Tubby said emphatically.

"Hard labor, huh? What about for murder?"

"Depends, could be the death penalty."

"You hear that, guys?" LaRue crowed. "Which do you figure is worse?" he asked Tubby.

No comment.

"I see it that way myself," LaRue said. "Makes it easier to figure out what to do with you."

"I don't even know who you men are," Tubby said. "What's your problem with me? I mean, what did we ever do to you?"

Peals of laughter came from the card table.

"You got some dumb luck," Monk cried.

"I'd like to ask your legal opinion about something else," Rue said. "Come over here."

"Like how?" Tubby asked.

"Oh, yeah." LaRue smiled. "Kind of hard to walk with your feet tied, isn't it."

He crouched to untie Tubby's legs.

"I don't want to have to kick you in the nuts again," LaRue warned. He had always found this to be an effective threat.

It worked with Tubby.

LaRue put an arm under the lawyer's shoulder and helped him stand.

"We'll leave your hands tied so you don't get too frisky. Because if you try anything I will mess with the girl. You hear that, Monk?"

He turned his back, and Tubby followed him into the bedroom, limping awkwardly. It was not so easy to walk straight with his hands behind him.

LaRue took a seat on the bed, settling down so lightly that the mattress did not seem to notice him. It struck Tubby that this man was something between a goat and a ghost. He couldn't help but notice the sparkling stones and stacks of cash spilling out of the two stuffed bags by the foot of the bed.

The card players in the next room were insulting each other about something. LaRue was feeling totally in control. "You remember when we met before, attorney-at-law?" he asked.

"I have no idea. Why don't you tell me?" Tubby took a seat on the other bed. "They call you Roux?"

"Yeah."

"Like when you make a roux for gumbo?"

"Something like that," LaRue said. He turned away to burrow out some papers he had stuffed under the pillow.

Tubby came off the bed like a bull out of the chute.

The thin, surprisingly strong man repelled him in a second, jamming the lawyer back into the mattress with a tight hand squeezing the cords of muscle in Tubby's neck. LaRue used his other hand to screw his pistol into Tubby's gaping mouth, causing him to gag.

"You need a killer instinct to get me, buddy, and you ain't got it," he said, breathing heavily.

Tubby fought to inhale. "I've done it before," he wheezed.

LaRue jerked his fingers off the lawyer's throat, leaving red marks, and Tubby's breath exploded from his wide-open mouth.

"You're gonna tell me you killed someone in the Army, aren't you," he said, leaving his pistol suspended above Tubby's face and straddling the lawyer on the bed.

"Not in the Army," Tubby said, looking up at the hole in the blue steel.

"Sure. Tell me about it," LaRue said. "I'll be your counselor."

Tubby shook his head, but not too much.

LaRue jumped off him and pointed his gun away.

"You might live to talk about this if you can help me. I want to know what something is worth. A legal document. Explain what it means and I might let you walk out of here."

"For how much money?" Tubby moved his eyes to the bags of stolen treasure. He didn't actually believe "Roux."

LaRue laughed and twirled the pistol around on his finger.

"Like how much money would my help be worth?" Tubby continued. "How much money?" He rubbed his index finger and thumb together behind his back. "Dinero," he added.

"You got brass balls, I'll say that." LaRue leaned back. "I guess it has a lot to do with how smart you are. If you can't answer my question I don't need you for anything."

"I'm smart enough to get paid for my advice," Tubby said.

LaRue's laugh might have lasted half a second. "So, what'll it be?" he asked.

"So what's your question?" Tubby leaned back on his elbows and waited.

"Move over here," LaRue said. He had some papers in his hand, and he gestured for Tubby to sit beside him. "Tell me what you make of these."

Since the lawyer's hands were out of service, LaRue unfolded the document carefully and held it a foot from Tubby's face, waiting impatiently for him to read it.

"Back that up a tad," Tubby said. "I'm a little farsighted."

"How's that," LaRue asked.

"Better."

He was looking at a Notarial Act styled, simply, "Counterletter." It had been executed in the Parish of Plaquemines in the Year of Our Lord Nineteen Hundred and Fifty-two, in the Year of Our Independence One Hundred and Seventy-six.

The eye-opener was that it appeared to be an agreement between two men who had large reputations—Noel Parvelle, who had made a fortune in the Cajun spices business, and Russell Ligi, who had gotten as rich as Midas from oil wells and politics. Ligi was also a recognized benefactor of the Lady of Lourdes All-Girls Soccer League, where about half of the kids in town, including two of Tubby's daughters, had learned the essentials of sportswomanship.

"You'll have to flip the page," he said, and LaRue did so.

Now this was interesting. Notwithstanding the fact that certain corporate records would reflect that Mr. Ligi owned a hundred percent of the stock of the Great Return Land and Investment Company, and all of its immovable property, tangible and intangible, the document in front of Tubby's nose stipulated that in truth and in fact eighty-five percent of those shares really belonged to the "Spice King," Noel Parvelle.

"One more time," Tubby said, and LaRue flipped another page.

Mr. Parvelle was entitled, if it were ever necessary to quiet title to any real property and mineral rights owned by the company, to record this counterletter in the public records. But clearly, the purpose of this counterletter was to keep the true ownership of the company hidden from the public's eye.

"Hmmm," Tubby said, wanting badly to scratch his chin.

"So, what's it mean?" LaRue asked, lowering the page.

Tubby told him.

"Is it any good?" the robber asked casually, folding the papers and putting them back in his pocket.

"Depends on what you mean by good."

"I mean, is it legal?"

"A counterletter? If I'm not mistaken they've been legal in Louisiana since the time of Napoleon. You're entitled to hide your business from the public."

"That don't sound proper," LaRue said sourly.

Tubby tried to shrug. "Look, you mind taking this rope off my wrist? It hurts like hell, and I'm surely not going anywhere."

LaRue shook his head. "You wouldn't think a piece of paper would be so important," he said.

"I imagine it could be very important to Mr. Parvelle," Tubby said. "If the Great Return Land and Investment Company is worth anything, Parvelle can record this document anytime he feels like he isn't getting his fair piece of the pie and take control of the whole company."

"You ever heard of it?" LaRue asked.

"No," Tubby said truthfully, but that didn't mean anything. There was lots of oil and gas property in south Louisiana, owned by lots of companies you never heard of.

"Me either," LaRue said, "but we went to a lot of trouble to get this paper."

Tubby was wondering exactly what "trouble" "Roux" and his helpers had gone to, other than shooting Mrs. Lostus, to acquire the mound of jewels on the floor.

"You was the one out in the flood with the woman, wasn't you?" LaRue asked, staring directly into Tubby's eyes.

"I don't have any idea what you're talking about," Tubby said, staring back.

Rue was impressed and grinned, showing Tubby his long pointy incisors.

"Yeah, that was you. You were just dressed different. Just gives me more of a reason to off you."

"I thought we were talking about payment in cash. You could probably use a good lawyer in the future," Tubby suggested hopefully.

"Not if you're never going to get caught." LaRue stood up.

"Sure, that's what you think now. And how about investment advice? You don't want to throw your money away." Tubby nodded at the canvas bags.

"What?" Rue laughed. "Are you offering your services?"

"You won't find any better."

"You're a slick son of a bitch, I'll hand you that. But don't try to hustle a hustler."

There was a light rap on the bedroom door, and Marguerite stuck her head in. Her eyes took in the shiny stones and lit up like flashbulbs.

"Mr. Rue," she said nervously. "There's some people on the street calling for Tubby Dubonnet."

LaRue bounded across the bedroom and knocked Marguerite aside.

Big Top was at the window, peering through the slats, and Monk was pressed behind the door. Edward and Wendell were frozen at the table, still holding their cards.

Someone was rapping on the shutters.

"Tubby Dubonnet?" A woman's voice.

"Look out!" Tubby cried from the bedroom, and caught his mouth on Willie LaRue's elbow.

Rue pulled his gun back out and with three quick strides he was at the cracked green shutters. They were fastened together by a bent iron hook. Rearing back, he kicked them open with the heel of his boot and stepped into the drizzly daylight, pistol ramrod-straight at his waist.

A big man in a hotel uniform was caught flatfooted on the steps. He waved his arms in the air, uncertain which way to jump. A female dove to the sidewalk on LaRue's left, fighting to get a pistol out of her pants.

The cowboy started shooting, going first for Dan's starched and ruffled white belly, where he left a round red stain, and then for the woman leaping for cover. She, however, was shooting back.

LaRue dodged back inside the apartment. The green wood above his head splintered. Fox Lane scuttled down the sidewalk like a crab on a beach and rolled around the corner of the building.

She peeked around quickly enough to see the man with the gun jump off the steps and take up a secure position behind a parked car. He rose and fired at her head, knocking mortar into her hair and eyes. He was calling out orders. She heard him tell someone to grab the bags and follow him.

Monk and Big Top bowled Tubby over in their haste to get into the bedroom and grab the loot.

Big Top looked once, then leapt like a paratrooper out the door, clutching one of the heavy sacks to his bosom. Monk started to follow but jerked back, squeezing his suddenly bleeding shoulder in agony where one of Fox's bullets had caught him. He let the bag drop and, bawling like a baby, dove out the doorway.

Tubby hobbled over to the top of the steps to look out, twisting and tearing his wrists against the ropes.

Every time Officer Lane poked her head around the edge of the mildewed brick, LaRue fired at her. Then he didn't, and she saw three men, using the parked car to shield themselves from view, running down the street. They were going in the direction of the river, and Monk was trailing. Tubby stumbled onto the top step, looked down, and let out an anguished howl.

At his feet, Dan was keeled over on his back with a red bubbling hole in his stomach. His blue eyes were open and staring heavenward at the black clouds blowing high over New Orleans on a wind from the west.

Tubby fell down the steps and dropped to his knees. Fox ran toward them, holstering her gun.

"Is he alive?" each asked the other desperately.

"I think he's breathing," Tubby said, and the broad chest suddenly jerked.

"He needs an ambulance," she cried. "Call nine-one-one!" she screamed at the woman standing above them in the doorway. Marguerite put her hands to her mouth and backed up, disappearing inside.

"Anybody else in there?" Lane asked.

"No more bad guys," Tubby panted. "Cut me loose!"

Even while she was digging in her pocket for her Swiss Army knife, Tubby started running clumsily in pursuit of Rue. The police officer had to cut the ropes while they were in motion, and she chopped off a few nuggets of skin in the process. Tubby picked up the pace when his numb hands swung free. He got his arms pumping and raced full tilt down Governor Nicholls Street.

"Stupid man," Fox spat through gritted teeth as she sprinted to catch up to the lawyer while at the same time trying to jam a new clip into her 9mm.

Puffing, Tubby had a fleeting glimpse of Monk and Big Top hustling around a corner in the French Market. Some visitors to the Quarter, attracted to the shots as they would be to any other pyrotechnic entertainment on a dreary holiday, got in the way, and Tubby pushed them roughly aside.

"I'll be damned. Watch where you're going," one of them said in dismay.

Fox caught up with Tubby just before he got to Decatur

Street, and got a grip on his shirt collar. She pulled hard on the reins just as he reached the corner and forced her way past him. She saw Big Top's red hair and hints of the two others vanish behind a row of produce trucks and stacks of crated vegetables.

"You stay here," she ordered. "I'm going around the market that way and catch 'em when they come out." She streaked away to her right, dodging some tomato vendors who were passing the time sipping coffee and eating hot sausage sandwiches on a wooden box of onions.

"No, I'm going this way," Tubby called to her retreating figure. He took a gulp of wet sea air and splashed across the parking lot toward the gap in the line of trucks where Big Top had last been seen. He worked his way between empty vehicles and found himself in the old open-air farmers' market. The stalls were mostly closed and covered with plastic. He thought he heard the sound of fleeing footsteps on the pavement flanking the river side of the market and ran in that direction.

A fog obscured much of North Peters Street. Tubby heard a muffled shot and followed the sound, hugging the side of the concrete floodwall for protection. A sudden gust of wind parted the mist, and he saw Monk lying down in the rain-washed street, curled in a fetal position behind some trash barrels.

A ferretlike man, unmistakably the one called "Roux," with Big Top on his heels, was snaking up the concrete steps that led over the floodwall. Both figures went over the top and were quickly hidden from sight.

Tubby puffed after them, leaving Monk on the ground where he was for Detective Lane to apprehend. The wounded robber heard Tubby running behind him and rolled over to watch him trot the steps. When Monk rolled back around he found the policewoman pointing a gun at him between the garbage cans.

"Oooh," he moaned, "you got me. Can you help me with this shoulder? I'm bleeding to death."

Tubby peered cautiously over the top of the floodwall. He could make out LaRue and Big Top running along the railroad tracks, past a string of rusty orange Public Belt railcars which appeared to be empty but for some vagrants camping out in relative dryness. Big Top had one of the canvas bags on his shoulder. Beyond the two running men, the Mississippi River rode high and swift against the bright green grass of the levee. Unlike the city, the river was not close to overflowing.

Panting down the steps in pursuit, Tubby began to consider his situation. He was unarmed and alone, chasing a pair of murderers at close quarters in a section of the riverfront that, save for a few pot-smoking street freaks, was deserted on this wet Mardi Gras afternoon. One such inhabitant, perched cross-legged on an overturned olive oil can, stared at him dully and suspiciously, but not especially unpleasantly. She tugged at a loose strand of her hair as Tubby huffed past. Two other gentlemen who were closer to Tubby's age rested on a railroad tie. They passed a joint and nodded vaguely at him in possible recognition.

Tubby hoped that Fox Lane had by now captured Monk and might soon be catching up with him. Otherwise this chase might end up with his own blood on the tracks. The path that LaRue and Big Top had taken was parallel to the river and might soon have them in Jackson Square, where tourists were certain to be more plentiful, and where they could probably get lost in the crowd.

Jackson Square did not, however, appear to be their immediate objective. Rue hopped over the railroad tracks and jogged up the side of the grass levee with Big Top's head hippity-hopping a few paces behind. Though one of the men was burdened by a sack of valuables, they were increasing their distance from Tubby. His musician's boots, though excellent protection against the rocks in the railroad bed, were beating the hell out of his feet. He was also not in training for competitive running, and only the blind rage caused by the red spot on Dan's shirtfront had gotten him this far.

A pistol crack sent Tubby headfirst into the dirt. He crawled on all fours for the protection of a rough wooden planter built to draw tourists in this direction on sunnier days. It had once held gardenias but more recently had become somebody's bedroom.

Edging his nose along the side of the rugged timbers, he found a crack stuffed with a discarded baby diaper. Removing it gingerly, he had a view of Big Top and Rue jumping from rock to rock at river's edge in the distance.

He could see a tugboat, painted red, black, and white, churning water against the Esplanade Wharf. The swollen river itself was almost empty of boat traffic. Its gray expanse blended into an overcast sky, which even the seagulls had abandoned for stations on the wooden piers under the docks.

LaRue and Big Top clambered up onto the wharf accompanied by screeches of these same birds, and they ran for the tugboat. If Tubby had had a hunting rifle, he could just about have popped them at this range. But he didn't.

Big Top, bag and all, leapt from the dock to the deck of the vessel below.

LaRue was telling him to put the ladder up for him, and Tubby started running toward them again.

Big Top got the ladder in place and LaRue started climbing down. He saw Tubby lumbering down the planks of the wharf and he calmly sighted his .45 down the rough creosoted surface.

A wave caused the tugboat to lurch, and with it the ladder. LaRue's shot went wild, but Tubby prudently fell flat again. LaRue jumped for the deck and pulled the ladder with him.

In the cabin, drinking coffee, Captain Ambrose thought he heard a loud noise, but over the thunder of his twin screws he couldn't quite be sure. He had them turning at two knots against the current just to keep the boat in one place beside the quay wall. He was not even tied up to the pier because he did not plan to be here long. His mate had just gone ashore to escort his girlfriend and Captain Ambrose's wife back to their cars. The two ladies had slipped on board Sunday night, and would have gone home yesterday had not the flood cut them off from their vehicles. With the city under water, the river was the safest place to be.

The captain had been sweating their presence ever since, because having a woman, even your wife, on board violated a large number of company regulations—especially if you were supposed to be working. And yesterday he had been working nonstop to secure a harborful of big oceangoing ships to safe moorings in the port as the river rose higher and the wind blew harder.

Both women had been forced to hide belowdecks in the kitchen, where they played cards, read his able-bodied seaman's *Playboy,* and got in a big argument about whether you put tomatoes in jambalaya. They were very cranky by Tuesday afternoon, and Captain Ambrose was so wired by then that he had even put a nasty dent at the waterline of a freighter. Someone was bound to notice it sooner or later. Now, a day after he had expected, he was finally rid of both of them. And if only his mate would hurry up and get aboard he could get this vessel back onto the river where it was supposed to be.

He heard footsteps rapping up the stairs from the galley below.

"Harley, that you?" he asked. "Fix us some coffee."

But the face that came through the hatch door belonged to some skinny wharf rat he had never seen before.

"Who do you think you are?" Captain Ambrose bellowed. Then he saw the gun in LaRue's hand.

"Shut up, shithead." LaRue coughed, advancing into the cabin. He was out of breath and getting that sleepy feeling.

Staggering up the stairs behind him was a redheaded man trying to get a gun out of his plaid Bermuda shorts.

LaRue pointed to the controls arrayed on the polished mahogany console.

"Get this boat out in the river," he commanded. "We're taking a ride. Do as you're told and you won't get hurt."

"You ain't allowed in the boat," Ambrose snarled.

LaRue stuck the barrel of the pistol in his face.

"You got any family?" he asked.

Ambrose bit his lip, thinking he did have a wife he loved pretty damn much even though she had been a major pain in the ass for the past thirty-six hours.

"All right," he said grumpily, swiveling around to his control panel. "Where ya wanna go?"

"Upriver, and fast," LaRue directed.

The captain pushed on a chrome lever with an orange ball on top, and the chugging below grew in volume. The floor throbbed.

Tubby meanwhile was running across the wharf and waving at Fox Lane, whom he could see coming on foot over the levee, to hurry up. As the tugboat started to rumble away from the pier, Tubby took a giant leap and crashed onto the deck.

He lay there in a heap for more than a minute as the boat roared back from the dock, too blue to move. His clearing vision enhanced the pain, and he decided his skull was cracked. His face, pressed into the corrugated steel, was on fire. But he wanted to tangle with "Roux." It was a compulsion to hurt someone such as he had not felt since he'd wrestled for his alma mater and old Coach Rugg had worked him into a frenzy at the state championship, urging him to tear every son of a bitch apart.

Tubby got himself into a sitting position and rested his head against the cool steel wall. Fox Lane's silhouette was getting smaller on the shore. She had her hands by her chin—radioing for help, he hoped.

Captain Ambrose watched the dock recede with mounting anger. Taking the *Prissy Ann* out against the current at near-flood stage was only moderately hazardous, but it used up lots of diesel, and it was something he usually got paid for.

"Where y'at, Ambrose? Over," his radio crackled. It was Robin at the office. The captain reached for the transmitter and switched it on.

"Leave it alone. Don't answer," LaRue ordered.

Big Top was entranced by all the lights and gauges.

"What happened to Monk?" LaRue asked him.

"He got shot in the arm and couldn't run no more."

"Who's that on board, Ambrose?" the radio inquired.

Ambrose looked over his shoulder at LaRue. "You realize this is piracy," he said. "And this here is the Port of New Orleans. That makes it a Loosiana crime."

LaRue bent down and put his nose next to the captain's.

"Shut up," he said quietly. He extended his hand and flipped off the transmitter. "Get cute with me again and I'll sink your damn boat. You can believe that."

"Monk dropped one of the bags of stuff," Big Top said dejectedly. "I couldn't carry them both."

LaRue looked through the glass over the bow, which was parting endlessly repeating black-edged waves. Approaching in the distance were the twin spans of the Crescent City Connection, looming like medieval castles guarding a mountain pass.

"Get in closer to shore," LaRue directed. "This ain't gonna be a long ride."

The sound of the weather deck door grating open below caused LaRue to step quickly to the top of the stairs. He saw nothing, so he opened the aft door on the bridge and stepped outside of the cabin where he could look down on the deck. The wind whipped his hair around and made his eyes water.

He saw that asshole Dubonnet scampering around the back of the boat to hide. LaRue fired once, sending a bullet whanging off the side of the pretty steel tug and into the vastness of the river. Carefully, he inched down the exterior stepladder to the deck.

As directed, Captain Ambrose pointed his boat toward the spire of the St. Louis Cathedral, and the *Prissy Ann* began digging through the murky deep toward the tourist overlook where stevedores had once loaded half the world's cotton onto steamboats.

When he saw LaRue descend out of sight on the ladder, the captain seized his opportunity. He grabbed the red whistle handle that dangled just above his head and gave it a good pull. An earsplitting "BZOOOOO" escaped from the air horns on top of the tug.

Big Top spun around spasmodically in search of the source of the ungodly sound, and Captain Ambrose took full advantage of his lack of vigilance. He lifted the massive brass handle off the directional finder and slammed it with a mighty "Hunh" against the back of Big Top's head.

The blow added momentum to Big Top's rotation but did not entirely brain him. He dropped his gun to the floor with a clatter but had enough survival instinct to grab the handle of the door to the outside where LaRue had gone, pull the lever, and reach open air.

Ambrose jerked his craft hard astern to avoid colliding with the boulders piled up to protect the shoreline. The lurch sent the addled red-haired robber tumbling mindlessly down the steps. He screamed and splatted onto the deck below.

Captain Ambrose heard someone coming up from the galley. Crouching down, he picked up Big Top's gun, ready to plug whoever came through the hatch.

"Whoa!" Tubby yelled, coming face-to-face with a crimson-cheeked seaman pointing a small cannon at him.

"Who are you?" Ambrose demanded.

"I'm a lawyer," Tubby said, hands up.

Ambrose shook his head in puzzlement. He had never let a lawyer aboard his boat before.

With a menacing curl of his lip he gestured for Tubby to advance, which he did in a rush when another gun fired from somewhere below them and a bullet hole appeared in the overhead of the cabin.

"That sorry bastard!" Ambrose screamed. "Quit shooting in my boat."

"Lemme use that gun," Tubby begged. "I'll go down and keep him busy, and you get us back to the dock. Call the police on your radio."

Ambrose was not used to having so many things go wrong at once in his floating kingdom, but he had not survived working on the river for twenty-five years because he flaked in a crisis. Snarling, he tossed the pistol to the lawyer and returned to his controls with both hands busy. He set a course for the most immediate mooring, where the steamboat *Natchez* was berthed.

Tubby, gun extended in front of him, began a slow, quivering descent to the galley.

At the bottom he jumped across the open space and cased the room from a half-crouch.

The weathertight door to the outside deck was open and swinging in the wind, and Tubby cautiously stuck his head through.

He saw LaRue bent over Big Top's body.

The robber squirmed around and placed one shot into the metal plate half an inch from Tubby's forehead, and Tubby stepped into the open and fired back. The bullet might have hit the unconscious Big Top or might have struck a Creole cottage a mile away, but it clearly missed its target.

The canvas sack was on the deck between them.

With Captain Ambrose again blowing his air horn in protest, LaRue ripped the diamond necklace off Big Top's chilly neck, and stood to face Tubby, gun to gun, mano a mano.

"You're empty," LaRue said.

"Doubt it," Tubby wheezed. He aimed at LaRue's midsection and pulled the trigger.

Loud click. Tubby looked dully at his weapon.

"I ain't," LaRue said.

Driven by instinct alone, Tubby hugged his head with both hands and jumped over the side. The roiling brown water of the Mississippi reached for him, then surrounded him with cold.

The *Prissy Ann*'s throbbing screws whipped him down, around, over and up, and through no power of his own he was expelled to the surface gulping for air.

Through the blond hair pasted over his forehead he glimpsed the spire of St. Louis Cathedral above the waves and began swimming furiously for the shore.

Helpless in the tugboat's wake, he washed against the rocks underpinning the levee. He hugged one, tried to stagger over it, and fell. He reached the Moon Walk by crawling.

Hippies dressed as one-eyed undertakers helped him ashore and laid him out on the warm timbers. He choked and heaved and blew off his nearly lethal dose of water like a beached whale.

An anxious sampling of local citizenry formed around him, offering freely their advice and opinion in a medley of dialects and languages from around the globe.

In a surprisingly short time, Tubby found that his faculties responded to the helm, and he tried standing up to the accompaniment of an impromptu blues band that was striking up a tune on the benches beside him and passing the hat. In fact, after all that running, the dip seemed to have done him some good. Smiling sheepishly and thanking everyone, Tubby broke through the circle of curiosity-seekers and climbed up the steps to see what had become of the *Prissy Ann*.

She was against the dock, not more than a hundred yards away, churning the river steadily near the stern of the steamboat *Natchez*.

Tubby hurried in that direction, and the imperturbable captain watched his approach from high on the tug's bridge.

"Can you grab a piece of line and tie us off?" Ambrose yelled at Tubby. "Or are you a fucking pussy?"

Tubby was a fucking pussy, but he helped to get the boat tied up. Captains evidently never did that kind of shit. Afterwards, adrenaline wearing off, Tubby also took off his wet shoes all by himself and lay down on the wharf to rest, all by himself. He was watching a pair of seagulls float lightly on currents of air when Fox Lane and a much larger policeman cantered up on a strong bay mare.

The uniformed officer put his hands around Fox's waist and lifted her off the horse tenderly. She looked up, smiling, and said thank you. She was also glad to see Tubby.

"The main guy, 'Roux,' got away," Tubby complained. "He took the money with him."

"At least I got the black dude," Fox said. "He's in the custody of this officer's partner. What did you say your name was?" She looked up.

"Reginald," he said, smiling down from the saddle.

"The other one, the redheaded guy, is down on the deck. I think he's dead," Tubby said.

That took the smile off Reginald's face, and he dismounted. His steed lowered its head, snorted, and grazed around for hot dog buns and novel smells on the creosoted wharf.

"He's not dead," Fox called out. She was down on the deck, kneeling over Big Top. The uniformed cop climbed down to look over her shoulder. He began talking on his radio. Tubby was six feet above them, on dry land, and he had no intention of returning to the boat.

"Ah, man, Rue," Big Top said softly.

"Is his name 'Roux'? Was he the guy in charge?" Fox asked.

"He stole my damn diamonds," Big Top said. His eyes were not looking at anything.

Reginald took his radio away from his ear.

"They lost him in Jackson Square," he reported. "An officer had him in sight, but he started throwing jewelry and money at people. Sounds like he started a riot and then beat feet."

Fox shook Big Top's shoulder.

"What's his name? Where did he go?" she repeated.

"I know where he went," Big Top said dreamily. "What's the name of that river up by the lake?"

"River?"

"Bayou St. John?" Tubby's voice came from above.

"That's it," Big Top said happily. "Across from a golf course. That's where he was supposed to meet 'em."

"Meet who?"

"Hell, how would I know? That's where we was to go to get paid." Big Top coughed. "My head hurts like the devil."

"We got an ambulance coming," Reginald told him.

"Whew," Big Top said, and expired.

23

"You missed him by half an hour," Wendell told Tubby. He and Edward were straightening up the mess in the apartment and taking an inventory of their clothes. "It took a long time, but the ambulance finally came and got your friend."

"His name is Dan," Tubby said. "Where did they say they were taking him?"

"Charity Hospital, I'm pretty sure they said."

"Where's Marguerite?"

Wendell avoided Tubby's gaze and busied himself with his broom.

"She left right after the ambulance did," he said finally.

Tubby stroked his chin. Then he brushed past Wendell and left a new trail of muddy footprints into the bedroom. It was just as he had left it an hour and a half before, except that there was no sign of any stolen property or any canvas bag.

He turned to find Wendell watching him from the doorway.

"Where's the bag of stuff?" Tubby squeezed Wendell's arm above the elbow. He noticed Edward kicking back in an armchair, hands clasped over his stomach, watching the cobwebs on the ceiling.

"Uh, what bag?" Wendell said, squirming against the pressure of the fingers gripping him.

"Don't give me that crap," Tubby said, squeezing harder.

"Your ladyfriend took it," Edward called.

"She just took it?" Tubby said incredulously.

"Acted like it was hers," Edward said.

"You mind letting go of my arm?" Wendell asked.

"Sorry," Tubby said, letting go. "How did she get it out of here?"

"Just carried it out on her shoulder," Edward told the ceiling.

"I don't believe that for a minute," Tubby said.

"Of course, I didn't really pay attention," Edward said.

"Neither did I," Wendell agreed.

Tubby's hands rolled into fists and his eyes narrowed to slits. Then he closed them and almost laughed.

"Did she happen to say where she was going?" he asked.

Wendell shook his head. Edward shook his head.

"She said this was one vacation she was going to remember," Wendell added.

Fox Lane spent the last hours of daylight methodically trudging around the places where cars could pull off Wisner Boulevard to park beside Bayou St. John. Eventually she found an empty blue Ford Taurus sitting under a tall cypress tree. It was unlocked, and the ignition had been popped. There was mud all over the driver's seat. She had not a doubt that the vehicle would soon be reported stolen, and that this was the car the man Tubby called Roux had used to get from the French Quarter to this spot. Someone had picked him up here.

There were no other signs of her quarry, so she called downtown for a tow truck. If the Taurus didn't get stripped first, she could go over it thoroughly at the impound lot. She was willing to bet she would not turn up a damn thing.

All in all, it hadn't been a bad day though. Of the three men who might be charged with homicide, one was dead and one was wounded and in custody. Considering how much better this was than her department's old averages, she might even get a commendation from the chief.

Intensive care was a quiet place. The nurse in charge, seated in the center of a circular counter in the middle of a round room, kept Tubby in view from the moment the white door whooshed open until he presented himself at her desk.

"Dan Haywood?" he inquired.

"Are you a relative?" she inquired.

"I'm a friend of his, and his lawyer," Tubby said.

Satisfied, she pointed to a segment of the ward curtained off from view and asked him to please be very quiet.

Tiptoeing, Tubby pushed the stiff fabric aside and stared at a very sick man.

The face that was sticking out of the blue blanket was gray and pasty. Dan had tubes coming out of his nose and out of his inert, outstretched arm. There was so much equipment around him he looked like he was sleeping in a stereo store.

Tubby was following the curve of Dan's substantial gut

where he knew the bullet had gone in, when it suddenly rose and fell. The head shuddered, and the mouth exhaled. Then the body was still again.

"What's his condition?" Tubby asked the nurse as quietly as he could.

She was filling out a chart with a red pen and did not look up when she spoke. "He's listed as 'critical,'" she said. "For more information you'll have to talk to the doctors."

"Okay. Where are they?"

"Best bet is tomorrow morning around nine o'clock. They're all making rounds then."

"Well, I mean, is he going to live?"

"I hope so, sir. Critical means he has an extremely serious injury. All we can do is hope for the best."

"But, like, what are his chances?"

"I'm sorry, sir." She put down her pen and looked over the top of her glasses. "That's all I can tell you."

Tubby gave it up.

At the other end of the hall, a policeman sat on an uncomfortable plastic chair outside a closed door.

"Is the patient in there named Monk?" Tubby asked. Now that he was near the uniformed man, he realized that he was not a city police officer, but rather a deputy from the Criminal Sheriff's Department.

"Who are you?" The guard straightened up in the chair and thought about standing up.

"I'm a lawyer. Tubby Dubonnet. I'm trying to locate a prisoner named Monk who was shot this afternoon in the French Market."

"Are you his lawyer?"

"Probably not," Tubby said wearily.

"So." The jail guard jerked his thumb as in instruction to depart.

"Well, would you mind giving him this?" Tubby offered an ivory card on which his embossed name looked far more neat and elegant than he actually felt.

"If he wakes up," the guard said.

"You might tell him his partner, Big Top, got killed, and the man they were working for ripped the diamond necklace right off his neck."

Tubby left the hospital and walked through dark and almost deserted streets to retrieve his car. It was time to go home and see what kind of mess the water had left him.

Except for a neighbor's car stuck in the mud of his front lawn and some strange garbage cans lodged in his azaleas, his home was fine—or as fine as he had left it. He called his ex-wife, Mattie.

"Hello," she answered loudly.

"Hi, this is me. How are y'all making out?"

"We had two feet of water in the yard. It covered up the deck, but nothing got in the house. Collette got trapped in a cab and had to spend the night with total strangers. Two of her friends are here, too. We're all making pancakes and doing our toenails."

"What about Debbie?"

"She's fine. She's at Marcos's apartment. It's on the second floor. Their lights were out all day, and every time I talked to her she was in bed, so I guess the marriage is still on."

Tubby nodded. That was okay.

"Christine was trapped here all day with me," Mattie continued. "Everybody was wondering where you were. The kids were worried." She didn't say she had been.

"I was stuck in the French Quarter. Dan Haywood got me a room at the Royal Montpelier. But we got involved in something, and Dan got shot in the stomach. He's in intensive care at Charity."

"Got involved with something. Dan got shot?"

"Yeah. Me, I'm okay."

"What on earth happened?"

"It's a long story. Tell the girls to call me when they get finished with their feet." It was his story to tell, not Mattie's.

They hung up.

Tubby stripped his clothes off on the way to the bathroom and stepped into a hot shower. Half an hour later he slipped under the covers and fell asleep, a full glass of bourbon untouched beside his bed.

24

On Ash Wednesday the sun shone brightly in a cloudless blue sky and the world repented. Fresh breezes stirred the crape myrtle trees and lifted the flowers from the flattened grass. Children came out to play. Parishioners walked to church for their mark of Lent. The city was fresh and clean momentarily, excesses forgotten.

On Tubby's front doorstep, the *Times-Picayune* lay just as it should. He stooped down to get it and, standing up, breathed deeply an elixir of sea salt, blossoming trees, rotting leaves, and the bacon he had frying in the kitchen. But for the automobiles stranded in odd places, and the line of organic matter a foot up on the foundation of his house, there was nothing to suggest that yesterday the world had almost come to an end.

He settled down in the kitchen with a cup of coffee and chicory, five crisp strips of bacon, and a tomato he had picked up from the vegetable man on Nashville Avenue on Saturday—a long time ago. The headline on the front page was two inches tall and said, "MARDI GRAS WASHED OUT." All other stories of international significance were relegated to the back pages. Thankfully, however, the courts of Rex and Comus had converged.

Three people had died, one story reported, and a woman's body had been found lodged in the street drain grating near the end of Poydras where police K-9 dogs were trained. As an aside, two of the noble German shepherds had escaped drowning by sitting through the rainy day on top of their kennels. One had actually climbed a twelve-foot fence topped with razor wire to get to freedom. Damage was estimated in the hundreds of millions of dollars. The previously unsinkable French Quarter had taken a heavy hit, washing a century of crud from barroom floors. The railroad bed of the St. Charles streetcar was badly eroded, and RTA officials estimated that it would take an amount equal to the entire federal appropriation for the nation's mass transit program in each of the next six years to repair it adequately. Grant applications were in the works.

On the first page of the Metro section, he found his story.

"Local Land Company Sold to Graxxon," the headline read. It was always a little unnerving to realize that on Fat Tuesday, when virtually every governmental and financial institution in south Louisiana was closed, commerce continued in the rest of the world. In this instance, the Great Return Land and Investment Company, owner of approximately 28,000 acres of mineral-rich marshland in Plaquemines Parish and many oil and gas leases across the region, had announced yesterday that it had been acquired by Graxxon in a complex transaction that involved the transfer of all of its stock to a group of local investors and then the outright sale of the same assets to Graxxon. The sale price was not disclosed, but industry analysts speculated that Graxxon had paid cash and stock valued in excess of $125 million.

A spokesman for these same "local investors," prominent attorney Clifford Banks, who had been this year's King of the Imbeciles of Abyssinia—one of many krewes unable to parade due to the weather—was contacted at his home. "It was a golden opportunity for local businessmen," he said. "Old Russell Ligi was ready to sell the Great Return Company, and the investor group was able to acquire it at a reasonable price. The investors already knew, of course, about Graxxon's interest in the property, so they immediately turned around and sold it." Banks declined to give further particulars about the transaction or the identity of the local investors. Nor would he comment on reports that spice magnate Noel Parvelle had claimed to be the true owner of the Great Return Company. Reached at his home in Meraux, Parvelle stated, "There will be litigation over this. You can bet on it. I've been cheated. I own that company and can prove it."

Elsewhere in the section there was a piece headed "Major Heist at First Alluvial Bank, Generous Bandit Pleases Crowd," but Tubby was staring off into space, watching the ceiling fans revolve.

In time, that lost its novelty so he dialed information to get Noel Parvelle's number. He made his call. Mr. Parvelle was quite agreeable to talking to him and suggested that Tubby drive right out to the parish and, "I'll tell you some story."

• • •

The old Creole lived in a big house with vast porches in the middle of a green cow pasture. It looked like open country, but if you knew how close the Gulf of Mexico lay to the backyard, you would wish for more elbow room. Parvelle would also have a nice view of the Mississippi River from his verandah, or at least a view of the forty-foot-high levee curving in the distance.

He was waiting for Tubby on his front porch, fastened into a wheelchair and highly agitated. He wore a green checkered shirt and a blanket over his legs, and his round, leathery face was the color of a boiled crab.

Tubby climbed out of his fat Chrysler, and while he was still crossing the yard the old man was yelling that he had been robbed by Russell Ligi. In the middle of his tirade he told Tubby to sit down beside him and said let's hear it.

He didn't wait but asked, "Do you know that bastard Ligi?"

Tubby sank down into a worn white oak rocker.

"No, sir. I've never met him."

"What the hell are you here for then?" Parvelle demanded, punctuating his syllables with spit. There were gaps in his teeth. He was chewing a great cud of tobacco, and the corners of his mouth were coffee-colored. He had all his hair though, and reminded Tubby of a wild boar that had almost overrun him in the swamp one time.

"Whoa," Tubby yelled, because he thought Parvelle

might be deaf, he talked so loud. "Let me tell you why I called."

Parvelle's yellow eyes got bigger as Tubby outlined the events of the past two days. When he described seeing the counterletter that evidenced Parvelle's true ownership of the Great Return Land and Investment Company, the old man sat back and clapped his hands.

"Russell Ligi is as devious as the devil," Parvelle whispered in glee. "I'd hate to meet him in hell."

"Yes," Tubby said in his most soothing voice.

"Let me tell you about Russell Ligi," Parvelle continued. "Him and me got political jobs from Earl Long, that shows you how honest Ligi is. A dollar passes into Russell Ligi's hands and a dime is all that rolls out.

"But he kept his hands off anything that was mine because he knew I'd cut the damn things off at the wrist. I had an interest in several companies that did business with the state. Man, we poured some concrete. I sold 'em a ton of school desks. And that's how I got into the spice business. 'Cause a lot of my family owns land, and LSU agriculture school set 'em up to grow tomatoes and peppers and bottle that stuff."

Parvelle rocked harder.

"So the folks in Baton Rouge were gonna auction off all these oil leases. You know the state owns all these water bottoms out here." Parvelle stopped moving. His wrinkled arm stretched out and made a slow sweep of the horizon.

"It's all around us. You could hit oil or gas right under this house. You just got to drill deep enough. I wanted those leases, and Ligi knew the guy who could let me know what to bid. Only it had to be in Russell's name." Parvelle reached out and dug his fingernails into Tubby's wrist. "I did too much business with the state, you see, and it would have looked bad. Russell got his income direct from the public. So that's why we formed the"—Parvelle almost sang—"Great Return Land and Investment Company, owned by Mr. Russell Ligi. And I put up every penny of the money—including paying Ligi plenty for the use of his name."

"And you got what?" Tubby asked, shaking his hand loose.

"I got that damn letter."

"Well, I guess you ain't got it no more," Tubby said. "Is there a copy?"

"Hell no," Parvelle exploded. "Are you an idiot?"

"Who was the lawyer who prepared the letter? Maybe he's got a copy."

Parvelle shook his head. "That was 'Skinny' Wormser. He went to prison. He's been dead for years."

"Did you get any money from the company in all this time?" Tubby asked.

"No. Me and Ligi went our separate ways." Cruel memories crossed Parvelle's face. "We never put the land into production. We—hell, *I*. I was saving it. I told Ligi anytime he asked—I'm leaving that land to my children as their inheritance. He didn't have any say about it because I owned the company. He never would have dared pretend otherwise. He knew what I'd do to him."

"So why did he screw you now?"

"Because of this!" Parvelle pounded his fists on the rails of his wheelchair. "I can't get out of here to kill him. I'm stuck on this damn porch. I'd pay good money for the job."

"No, no, no," Tubby said quickly. "Not interested."

"I'll find somebody else," Parvelle said. "How are you going to make a buck off this then?"

"Well, uh, I don't know if I can."

"Someone made Russell do this," Parvelle said, staring past Tubby's head. "Somebody he's more afraid of than me. Because he knows I will kill him. Russell never would have thought about a bank robbery either. He doesn't have the brains or the balls. I'll pay you to find out who that somebody is."

"Maybe it's the local investors the newspaper wrote about."

"Yeah? And who are they?"

"The newspaper didn't say."

"And that's the way it's gonna stay. They going to be hard to find," Parvelle said.

Tubby left him soon afterwards. Driving back to New Orleans, he was thinking how fragile a handshake is. Even a handshake backed up by a legal document safely stored in the vault of a bank.

Tubby took a ride on his Harley to clear his head. In a moment of lunacy he had ordered the motorcycle months before, and he had only ridden it a couple of times.

He didn't feel he deserved it. It reminded him of a bad episode in his life, and truth was, he thought he looked funny on it. But then the governor got one, and even a television judge. By the time he hit River Road, speeding beside the grass-covered embankments of the levee, he didn't care anyway. Swooping around a long curve, flying under the Huey Long Bridge, what came to mind was a pretty face wrapped in straw-colored hair, a woman lying on a hotel bed, trying on his black boots, waving her legs in the air to admire them.

25

Marguerite stared past the long silver wing of the jetliner. Snow covered the ground as far as she could see. The pilot had announced just a second ago that they were on a path to land at O'Hare in thirty minutes. She had slept through most of the flight and dreamed about the man called Rue firing point-blank into the poor bellhop's stomach. A stewardess had noticed her squirming around and shaken her gently awake.

Marguerite had smiled weakly and accepted the offer of a ginger ale.

There was a canvas bag in the hold of the plane with her claim check on it. Unless the thieving baggage handlers at O'Hare stole it, Marguerite would soon be collecting a fortune. She would tip a redcap to cart the sack to a taxi. She had not yet figured out where she would hide her bounty once she got the bag home, but if they left her alone for even a couple of hours, she would come up with something. She always had been resourceful. One thing you learned in the commodities business was how to live on the edge.

The handsome lawyer with the broad chest came to mind,

and she smiled to herself. He definitely rated as unfinished business. Her race to gather her belongings from the Royal Montpelier and to depart New Orleans had prevented any goodbyes. If she managed to stay out of jail, however, she would look him up again. Meanwhile, Marguerite could imagine many wonderful things, like how her mother would cry for joy when her mortgage was finally paid off. Like her boss's expression when Marguerite said see you later, sucker. Straightforward as Marguerite was, it would be difficult not to tell her mother, or Rondelle, about the treasure, but change was what life was all about. A smart lawyer had told her that.

Edward and Wendell were strolling on Bourbon Street, drinking good beer from plastic cups.

"Can you believe how everything's changed? It's like there was never a flood, or anything," Edward said in awe.

The faces they passed were smiling. The sun was shining.

"It's like the whole city has been born anew," Wendell agreed.

"I just love it here," Edward said, pausing to look through a store window at the framed Jazz Fest posters being hawked for sale.

"It's been a great adventure," Wendell agreed. "You couldn't ask for a better Mardi Gras."

"We ought to think about moving here when we retire." Edward laughed.

"We could do that soon," Wendell said. His pockets were heavy with other people's trinkets.

"I'm afraid I'll have to give you a ticket," a pretty young woman said, blocking their path.

"What do you mean," Edward asked, highly alarmed.

"I have to give you a ticket for having too much fun." She winked. "And the ticket entitles you to a free gourmet lunch and a brand-new VCR."

"What?" he exclaimed. Edward was relieved beyond belief not to be under arrest.

"Honestly, all you have to do is take a tour of the Pirate Mansion. It just takes half an hour. That's not so bad, is it?"

"Exactly what are you selling?" Wendell asked.

"Great, affordable vacation apartments in New Orleans. We have weeks available all year round. And the accommodations are just beautiful."

"Time-shares," Edward said, grasping the proposition.

"Our van is right around the corner," the smiling lady said.

"Should we?" Edward asked.

"I think it might be fun," Wendell said.

26

Fox Lane called Tubby from the hospital to say that Monk was ready to talk, but only with a lawyer present. He had designated Tubby Dubonnet, who told the police detective he could meet her there in half an hour. She said fine, that would give her time to grab something to eat from the fruit man outside. She wouldn't eat the food at Charity Hospital.

He got held up finding a place to park near the medical center, like he always did, so it was more like an hour before he got off the elevator. He found his former classmate reading an old *People* magazine in the waiting area.

He asked how she was doing.

"Tired," Fox said, brushing some fragments of orange peel off her Levi's. "There was a drive-by shooting last night on Jackson Avenue and a five-year-old kid got killed." She shrugged.

"How do you do it?" he asked.

"How does anybody do their job? Come on." She led the way toward Monk's room.

"I'm doing an official interrogation, Tubby," she said over

her shoulder. "You're here as the suspect's lawyer." She was setting the rules.

"I want to talk to him in private for a minute then, to see if I'm going to represent him." He could set some rules, too. He had not thought of a way he could be a witness, victim, and lawyer in the same case yet, but he wanted those few private moments with Monk.

"Where's the damn guard?" she asked when they rounded the corner into the hallway. It was empty.

As if to answer her, the deputy in the black uniform appeared at the far end of the hall. He had a red can of Barq's in one hand and a pack of Cheetos in the other.

"Just getting me something to eat," he said, grinning.

"You're not supposed to leave him alone," Fox said sternly.

"He ain't going anywhere," the deputy said. "And mind your own business. You work for the police. I work for the sheriff."

Fox swallowed what she wanted to say. "Go on in, counselor," she told Tubby. "Please don't take all day. I've got work to do."

"Right," Tubby said. He opened the door, stepped inside, and let it close softly behind him. A limp cotton curtain separated him from the patient's bed.

"Monk?" he said.

No reply.

Tubby pulled back the curtain and froze. The blood was still dripping out of Monk's neck where his throat had been sliced open. His head hung at an angle off the side of the bed. His mouth was a wide hole, and there was a red stream over his chin, around his ear, and down to the floor, where it made a puddle containing all of Monk's life.

"Fox!" Tubby cried, and she was stiff-arming him out of the way.

A passerby might have mistaken the slightly disheveled lawyer sitting in the park for a patient at one of the nearby psychiatric institutions and the crisply dressed black woman in earnest conversation with him for his social worker. That would not have been far off the mark.

"It's just gotten to me," Tubby said.

"You haven't seen what I've seen, buddy," Fox said. She hunched over, hands clasped and elbows on knees, just like Tubby.

"There's far too much violence in this city," he said.

"Yeah, but nothing new about that."

"The thing is, there is something new here," Tubby explained fervently. "I'm feeling like there's some kind of evil hand at work all around us."

Fox looked at him sharply.

"Some kind of force that can set up a heist at a bank, that does deals with big oil companies, that can reach into a major hospital and kill a man. Somebody's pulling the strings."

He put his hand on her shoulder, then remembered she was a cop and took it off.

"I've lived in this city for more than twenty years," he said. "Almost everything I care about is here. I can't let him ruin it for me."

"What are you talking about, Tubby?"

"I know why they robbed the bank vault. It was just to get Noel Parvelle's counterletter. All the other stuff they took was just lagniappe. He needed that counterletter to put together his oil deal. He, they, the mastermind. They killed one, two, three people to get that letter. If Dan doesn't make it, that'll be another person they just whacked out of the way. I know the why, I just don't know the who."

"You're jumping around a lot, Tubby. You don't know all those things are connected."

"Hell, I know it, and you know it," he yelled. "There's a goddamn evil hand at work here."

"Oh, knock it off! Granted, there's always been someone behind the scenes calling the shots in New Orleans. That's how this place works. That's how it's always worked. But I wouldn't call it an 'evil hand.'"

"It hasn't always been this way," he insisted, too loudly. Seeing her expression, he lowered his voice. "Nobody's ever been allowed to steal anything he wants, kill anybody he doesn't like, and get away with it."

"Tubby, this is not like you. You're more, I don't know, reasonable than this."

"To hell with that. Dan is in the hospital. Mrs. Lostus is dead. Monk is dead. Darryl Alvarez is dead. Tania's brother is dead. Hell, they probably even killed Joe Caponata. You can't call this business as usual."

"What are you babbling about? I don't even know who half these people are," she said.

"Well, I do!" he shouted.

She shook her head and looked at the sandy dirt, the ants crawling over a lollipop.

"You're hopeless."

"Maybe, but I'm going to get the sons of bitches, whoever they are." There was great intensity in his voice.

"And what's any of this got to do with Joe Caponata's death? That old mafioso got run over by a car."

"Yeah? Yeah?"

"I don't think I've ever seen you excited like this. You were always the calm one."

"I haven't always played by the rules, Fox, but I've never screwed a client or lied to the judge. But that's just not enough to cut it anymore." He spread his hands helplessly. Then he looked away. "This has been a very disturbing year for me," he said, almost to himself.

"So take a vacation." The detective spoke softly.

"I'm just not in the mood for that kind of advice." Tubby fixed his eyes on hers.

"Suit yourself," she said, and stood up. "I've got to go to work."

Tubby followed her down the sidewalk.

"I'm asking you to help me with this," he told her back. "It might reach into Texas and the Gulf Coast. It could be national."

"You must think I'm as nuts as you are," Fox said. "You go messing around with some ol' evil hand and it's liable to snuff you out like a candle in church. I already saved your life once this week. I'm not gonna do it again."

That shut Tubby up, for a moment.

"I can't just take a vacation while the city I live in—supposedly the best and friendliest city anywhere—is being poisoned to death," he said finally, almost inaudibly.

"You're way too worked up." Fox had reached her car. She turned to face Tubby. "When I was a little girl, my mother used to sing a blues song. It went like this:

> "Dark green trees,
> Swaying in the summer breeze.
> Love's so sweet
> When strangers meet.
> Little baby cries
> Hearing young men's lies.
> Fish are cooking,
> My man's sure good-looking.
> I might be your Queen,
> Or your bad dream.
> Nobody ain't seen
> Mama's New Orleans."

"Your mother was a blues singer?"

"My mother was a homemaker. She raised us kids and never worked for anybody else. My father was a Pullman porter."

"'I might be your Queen'?"

"Those are the words."

"The point being, what?"

"You figure it out. The point being, you can dwell on what's good, or you can dwell on what's bad. There's plenty of both. But take it from a cop. You can't lift all the world's problems on your shoulders."

She got in her car.

"I think you'll feel better tomorrow. Really," she told him.

27

Finally, his feet were getting dry. Elvin could smell the leather of his old worn-out shoes baking where they leaned precariously up against a hunk of driftwood beside the fire. His socks, suspended in the smoke and flying sparks on a green willow branch, gave off a rich scented steam like a boiling fish. Above his head, the dense trees stirred, scattering stray droplets of yesterday's storm.

Elvin's simple camp in the woods by the river, near the headquarters of the Army Corps of Engineers, had taken a beating from the rain. The blue plastic tarp that provided his shelter had ripped loose from its bits of rope and flown like a great wounded bird through the jungle until it wrapped itself fast around a high cypress branch. It remained there flapping annoyingly at him.

His small store of usable clothes was drenched and muddy. What he regretted most was the loss of his two rolls of toilet paper—now sodden lumps covered with brown leaves. That and the toll two days of cloudburst had taken on his feet, which were itching to distraction, until finally he had managed to get his campfire lit with the help of a quart of motor oil he had swiped from the Corps.

Through the bushes he could watch a long line of blue barges being pushed upriver by a fiery red tugboat. The captain was looking at him, and at the smoke from his fire, but neither man acknowledged the other.

All of a sudden Elvin heard a branch snap behind him. Twisting his head in fear, he beheld not what he expected— some rangy dog set loose in the woods for exercise—but a thin figure of a man, peculiar ears protruding beneath a brown cowboy hat, held on by a green band he thought, standing motionless not five feet away and watching him with expressionless eyes.

"Ooh, scared me, neighbor," Elvin said, trying to quiet his own raspy breathing. He attempted to rise.

The strange man did not speak, and his gaze did not leave Elvin. Then, quick as a snake, he cocked back a length of tree branch and swung it like a baseball bat at Elvin's face. It connected solidly with a blast of pain. The vagabond fell to his knees and would have screamed but the branch fell upon his head again and again.

The bludgeoning continued until the features of Elvin's head were flattened and crushed together in a stew of red flesh. His lifeless form was then roughly lifted and dumped headfirst into the coals, causing a great eruption of sparks that danced away in the breeze as quiet returned to the woods.

Calmly, the tramp's attacker poured the remains of a can of oil over the body and watched the fire gain new life. Then he sat down on the log where Elvin had been resting and pulled off his own muddy boots. He laid them by the fire as if to dry and picked up one of Elvin's cracked brogans. He debated whether to put the stinking things on his feet or to just hike barefoot out of the woods. After he rested, that is. He felt very sleepy.

Detective Kronke was polite enough to interview Tubby at his office. The building was back in service again—elevators running and lights responding—though the halls were nearly empty. Many people were staying close to home, sorting out their private catastrophes.

Tubby's secretary, Cherrylynn, had not made an appearance. There was not even a message from her on his voice mail, which had him a little worried.

The policeman arrived alone, promptly at twelve o'clock, as he said he would. Tubby showed him the way in and invited him to sit on one of his leather chairs.

"Terrible flood," the detective observed, extracting a pad and pen from his pocket.

"Yes, it was," Tubby said. "How did you make out?"

"Personally? Oh, my car is shot for the second time in three years. All the rugs are going to have to come out of my house. Typical. You?"

"No real problem. Just water in my yard."

"I think it was worse downtown than out where I live in Gentilly."

"Possibly," Tubby agreed.

"Anyway, to the business at hand. I understand that you were kidnapped by a group of men who shot a woman passing in the street, and they also shot a man who was trying to rescue you. These are probably the same boys who broke into the First Alluvial Bank. I know you've already given your statement to Homicide. I'm just trying to find out what I can about the robbery."

Tubby listened in silence.

"As of now," the detective continued, "we do not have a complete list of what was stolen. The bank is still in the process of notifying its customers and so forth. They're supplying lists of what they claim was in the safe-deposit boxes. True? Who knows." Kronke shrugged. "Right now it doesn't look like very much will be recovered."

Tubby nodded.

"I am told that you saw some of the stuff that was stolen from the bank."

"Yes, if that's what it was. They had a canvas bag, and I saw some jewelry that looked like diamonds and some other things. It was all in a pile." The vague response did not seem to bother the cop.

"Now it looks like, when the leader of the gang was making his escape, he actually started throwing this jewelry around in Jackson Square. He created quite a mob scene."

"I wasn't there," Tubby said.

"No. You took a little swim in the river, didn't you?" The detective chuckled.

Tubby rubbed his eyes and recalled the weight of the waves closing over his head.

"Anyway, he got away," Kronke resumed. "And may or may not have escaped with any of his loot. Anybody who got their hands on any of the stolen property in Jackson Square got out of the area as quick as they could. Would you recognize this guy again?"

"Yes. No doubt. I gave his description to Fox Lane, and she ran it through the computer. She told me nothing came up."

"Yeah. Well, I guess I'm just covering the same ground. Now let's see—there were also two fellers and a woman taken hostage with you."

"Yes."

"These two men say that the only particular items they saw that might have come from the bank were a watch one of the bad guys had on and a diamond necklace another one had."

"Okay."

"As far as the woman, they say they don't know who she was. They say she came with you."

"That's right. She was someone I met at the Royal Montpelier the night of the flood. She gave me shelter from the storm. Her name was Marguerite. I'm not sure how you spell her last name. You could get it from the hotel."

"Yeah. I already did. She checked out and apparently went home to Chicago. I got her address from the credit card she used, and we'll be calling her. I don't expect her to tell us much except maybe what a sick city this is."

"No."

"You got anything to add?"

"Like what?"

"Hell if I know. None of this leads anywhere. We may just have to wait and see if anything turns up that we can identify as coming from the bank. Or maybe the guy who got away will trip up and get caught. Right now it's just more forms for me to fill out."

Tubby escorted the detective back to the door and watched him slouch down the hall to the elevators.

What was that son of a bitch really after? he asked himself. Is he part of it, too? Does he work for the guy who hired the crooks? Is he trying to find out what I know about Russell Ligi and his oil deal?

Too paranoid to stay long in one spot, Tubby locked his office up tight and hustled off to the parking garage where he could get his car and drive—anywhere.

28

The telephone rang too loudly.

"This is Fox," the voice on the other end said.

"I got up this morning, and I didn't feel any better," Tubby replied. He stared at his own bleary, unshaven face in the bedroom mirror. He had been about to go to bed.

"Maybe this will help. Your mystery-man cowboy is dead."

"Roux?"

"Or whatever his name is. Some bird-watchers found him in the hobo jungle on the other side of the levee near the Corps of Engineers. He'd been beaten to death and partly burned up in a bonfire."

"You're sure it was him?"

"The cowboy boots that you described were there. So was the hat with the green band, and the wet clothes. And so was an old pocket watch with the name Dubonnet etched on it."

"That's my grandfather's watch. I'm grateful that you found it."

"So, anyway, he's in the morgue."

"Have you learned his identity?"

"We've run what's left of his prints, but so far there's no match."

"Who killed him?"

"No idea yet, and we may not ever know. It could have been another sicko living down on the batture. It could have been somebody off a boat."

"It was probably the big-money people who planned this whole thing," Tubby said, his voice rising.

"Yeah, I guess that could be it, too." Fox sighed.

"Where do you go from here?" he asked.

"We'll keep the file open," she replied. He could visualize her shrugging. "But right now, Tubby, it's three for three. Everybody implicated in the murder of Mrs. Lostus, everybody involved in the assault on Dan Haywood, has now gone to their reward."

"And is burning in hell."

"Maybe."

"You know, don't you, there was more to it than those three men."

"Goodbye, Tubby."

"Thanks for calling."

He lay down and tried to fall asleep.

"Hello, Tubby?"

He recognized Marguerite's voice immediately, and it rescued him from a nightmare vision of a pile driver exploding downward about to pound him into the earth.

"Hello," he managed. His mouth was dry, and he was out of breath.

"I had a hard time finding your number."

"I'm glad you tried," he said, sitting up and checking the clock. It was three o'clock in the morning. "Where are you?"

"I'm in Chicago. How are you?"

"Not so good. My friend Dan, the bellman, is still in the hospital."

"I was afraid he might have, you know, died."

"No, but he's in a coma. All three of the crooks are dead though."

"Big Top and Monk?"

"Yeah, and the leader too."

"I don't care what happened to him, but I didn't really think the other two were so bad."

"I saw Big Top die. He got clocked on a tugboat and never recovered. Monk had his throat cut in a hospital. They haven't found out who killed him or Roux. It might be the people they worked for."

"There's someone else?" Her voice trembled a little.

"I think so," Tubby said. "I was sort of afraid they might be after you."

"Why me?" she exclaimed.

"There's the small matter of a missing bag of stolen property."

"Oh. That. A policeman called me from New Orleans. He didn't seem to know anything about the bag that got lost."

"Name of Kronke?"

"Yes."

"He talked to me," Tubby told her. "I didn't know whose side he was on, so I didn't give him anything. I didn't turn you in."

"What do you mean, whose side?"

"There are big people with big money behind all this. That's all I know."

She did not say anything, but he could hear her breathing.

"I'm glad you're safe," he said. Somewhere in the distance a dog was howling. A branch, stirred by the wind, scraped against his windowpane.

"I've missed you," she said.

"I thought you ran out on me."

"I was afraid you might think that. I was kind of outside myself, like almost in another body, after we were taken prisoner. But as soon as I decided what I was going to do, I knew I had to do it by myself. If anyone gets in trouble it should be only me."

"You think you'll ever come down to New Orleans again?"

"I just might. I've quit my job, and I guess I should go traveling somewhere. See the world. But right now, I'm going to cooking school."

"Really? What made you do that?"

"It's just something that came to me. I was remembering our special dinner in the hotel room. And I thought it was maybe something you would enjoy, if I ever saw you again."

Tubby felt some of his armor slipping away. Against his better judgment, a little ray of hope entered his heart. It had been a long time since he had had a real relationship with a woman—or even thought he could have one again.

"What does a chef in the Big Potato teach you? How to grade beef?" he asked.

"No, we cook other things." She laughed.

"Like Chicago-style pizza?"

"Yes, actually, but we also made a good Costoletta Valdostana yesterday, which is veal chop stuffed with prosciutto ham and Muenster cheese. And tonight we're cooking chicken fricassee."

"That sounds pretty good," Tubby conceded. "I guess the New Orleans versions would be veal grillades served with a nice thick gravy and something like Chicken Big Mamou in Pasta like Chef Paul makes."

"I'm not even going to ask what that is," she said. "The *pièce de résistance* we're making this week is supposed to be roast duck."

"My my," Tubby said. "You know, the best duck I ever had was at a restaurant in New Iberia where they served me these two grilled ducks, and they laid out a big helping of wild rice and some tasso dressing."

"What's a tasso?"

"It's like a smoked ham. Some people call it Cajun ham. You could use sausage probably."

"We've got plenty of that in Chicago. Bratwurst, knockwurst, Italian, blutwurst . . ."

"Now, that's like boudin. That's a Cajun blood sausage. You know, you're making me hungry."

"Gross. All that stuff is bad for you anyway. How are your daughters?"

"They're fine. Thank you for asking."

"I'd like to meet them sometime."

"I would want to get to know you a little better first."

"Maybe you could come up here."

"I'd like to, but I'm going to be busy for a while. I've got to find out what's happening locally. For my own satisfaction, if nothing else. I'm going to try and find out who is responsible for killing all of these people." And make them pay.

"That could take a long time."

"Maybe, but I feel like it may be my mission."

"It wouldn't hurt to take a weekend off."

"That's very tempting. I'll call you when I'm free."

"You're a hard guy to get a date with."

"I'll promise you this. The next date I go on will be with you."

"Gotcha," she said. "I'll even pay your way."

Tubby laughed.

"I'm quite rich," she added.

"Yeah? And how do you explain that?"

"Slot machines, honey."

"Are you paying your taxes to Uncle Sam?"

"You bet."

"Well, watch where you step."

"You too, dear. And I'll see you soon." He heard the sound of a gentle kiss, and he hung up the phone. He wanted to believe. It had been too long since there was a woman in his life he could trust. Marguerite might be a thief, but there was nothing deceitful about her.

29

Tubby lured his daughter over to his house after school on Friday with the promise of a motorcycle ride. They sat on the porch and drank iced tea first, and told each other about their Mardi Gras experiences.

"Do you know when Dan will get well?" Collette asked, eyes troubled.

"No." Tubby shook his head. "There's some kind of nerve damage, and he's not responding very well. It's just wait and see."

"The two of you were good friends in college?" she asked.

"Yeah. We both wrestled. You met him a couple of times when you were a baby, but you've forgotten about him."

"I sort of remember."

Tubby smiled. "Do you think you'll see Bradley again?" he asked.

"Oh, I don't know." She brushed a drop of water off her knee. "The way Mother acted around him, he may not want to ever come back."

"What do you mean?"

"Oh, she told all of the most embarrassing and stupid stories about me, and Christine, and Debbie, in that loud voice of hers, the one she always gets when she's been drinking."

"Well, it was Mardi Gras, after all."

"I don't really think that's much of an excuse," Collette said unforgivingly.

"Come on, that's an excuse for almost anything."

"It was a funny Mardi Gras," she mused.

"It sure was," Tubby agreed.

"Even with the flood and everything, it still seemed extra special, you know?"

"Yeah, like all of the important elements were there. The marching clubs, the Buzzards, the high school bands, the Indians. Even Rex made it. The spirit was still there."

"New Orleans certainly is a strange place," she said. "Sometimes I wonder what I would think of all this if I hadn't grown up here."

"No telling," Tubby said. "It would be a lot to absorb."

"Of course, people here drink way too much," she said.

"Yeah," her father agreed. "We've sure got some problems."

"The other places I've been seem so backward though."

Tubby raised his eyebrows. "You haven't really been to that many places," he pointed out.

"Oh, I realize that," she said. "But isn't New Orleans generally considered by most people to be a very, you know, progressive city?"

"Yes, I'm sure that's true," Tubby said wisely. Nobody could dispute a statement like that.

"Come on," he said. "Strap on that helmet and let's take

this baby out for a spin around our magnificent, littered metropolis."

Fox had been partly right, he thought as he settled his rump onto the wide leather seat and felt his daughter behind him get a good grip on his belt. When a bright sun came up over the City That Care Forgot, you did feel better in the morning. It was pretty here. Strange ladies smiled at you on the street. The air smelled good. Tubby could even make himself stop thinking about the evil force that was sucking the guts out of his town, if he tried. If he wanted to. Let the law handle it. Maybe the conspiracy was all just in his imagination anyway. It was fertile enough, God knows.

He could forget about finding the master crook, hiding behind the veil, up at the top of the heap, breathing the same sea-scented air.

But he didn't think he would. There was still a final mission to be accomplished.

Tubby cranked the engine and gave it a goose. The beast sprang for the street, and his daughter screamed in delight.

In a dark hospital room, Dan tried to wake up.